DAVY'S DREAM

Written and Illustrated
by
PAUL OWEN LEWIS

Published by:
Beyond Words Publishing, Inc.
Pumpkin Ridge Road
Route 3, Box 492-B
Hillsboro, OR 97123
Phone: 1-503-647-5109
Toll Free: 1-800-284-9673

Printed by Dynagraphics, Inc., Portland, Oregon
in the United States of America

First printing May, 1988
Second printing March, 1989

ISBN: 0-941831-28-0 Soft Cover
ISBN: 0-941831-32-9 Hard Cover

Library of Congress Catalog Number: 88-070816

For information about a school lecture and
slide show of Davy's Dream, please contact
Beyond Words Publishing.

Dedicated to the memory of my friend and father,
GARY BARTON LEWIS.
With thanks to Jasper,
Mimi, and C.B. Johnston.

One sunny afternoon,
a boy named Davy
lay in the tall grass
on a hilltop dreaming.

It was a dream of killer whales.

He saw himself sailing among them

in play,

in song,

in silence,

and in joy.

When he awoke,
he ran down the hill into the harbor town
eager to share his dream of the happy whales
with the people there.

"Ha, wild Orca? They're dangerous," laughed an old fisherman.

"Not like those tame ones doin' tricks."

"Yep, 'Wolves of the Sea' we call 'em around here," agreed another.

"Hunt in packs and eat anything," said yet another, squinting his eyes as he spoke.

Davy suddenly felt very foolish. He told no one else about his dream that day.

But the wonder he felt for the whales
and the memory of the dream
would not leave him.
He sailed out of the harbor
and into the straits
to look for them.

Not long afterwards,
far away on the water's surface,
he saw what looked like little black triangles.

Killer whale fins!

Quickly he trimmed the sails
and raced towards them.
Davy's hopes rose together with the
spray off the bow of the boat.
But, he could soon tell, the whales were
swimming away from him faster than
he could follow.

Once more he trimmed the sails.
Davy's hopes rose
as he raced towards them.
But at the last moment,
the whales dived — and vanished.

He tried again and again,
  but always it seemed the whales
  would have nothing to do
  with the boy in the boat.
  "I guess the dream
    was just a dream after all,"
  Davy said to himself.
  He sailed for home.

The next day,
　　Davy was bored and restless.
　　　With nothing better to do
　　he climbed back up
　his sunny hilltop to think.
As he sat,
　　the heat of the sun made him drowsy.
　　　He lay down in the grass,
　　　　closed his eyes,
　　　fell asleep,
　　and began
to dream again . . .

When he awoke,
he ran down into the town —
and telling no one . . .

Playing, singing, resting,
and jumping for joy together —
Davy and his new friends had done it all!
But now, the setting sun reminded him that it
would soon be dark. It was time to go home.
Davy waved goodbye,
and the whales each spouted in reply.

The evening air darkened quickly as the little
sailboat glided home alone. Then, without
warning, there was a loud

CRUNCH

and the boat lurched to a stop.
Davy knew at once he must have hit a rock
as water began to fill the boat.
The boat was sinking.

No sooner had he started bailing
when two towering black fins
rose out of the water
on either side of the boat.
The boat began to rise —
and move forward very fast.

In no time at all
Davy was safely back in the harbor.

The next morning, Davy told everything to the fishermen.

"Boy," said the first, "you've been watching too much TV!"

"Imagine that," said the second, "being rescued by wild killer whales. That lad can sure tell a good fish story!"

"Got a screw loose more likely," said the third, squinting his eyes as he spoke.

Davy left the men again.
But this time, a great big smile grew on his face.
Because he knew — and you and I know too —
that dreams can come true.

Planet
Awakening

Patricia Waak

D1534172

Audubon

"What Jesus Runs Away From" translated by Coleman Barks from *The Essential Rumi* copyright © Threshold Books. Used by permission.

Photo Credits:
Cover photo—Silhouette in Zimbabwe, Digital Imagery © Copyright 2000 PhotoDisc, Inc.
Page 7— The Earth © PhotoSpin Inc.
Page 8—Man Standing Atop Sand Dune, Death Valley, Digital Imagery © Copyright 2000 PhotoDisc, Inc.
Page 9—Bird Footpints in the Sand, Digital Imagery © Copyright 2000 PhotoDisc, Inc.
Page 10—Stars, PhotoSpin Inc.
Page 11—African Sunrise © 2000 Patricia Waak
Page 17—The photo of Thomas R. Malthus was taken from a copy of the original painting held by Jesus College, Cambridge. Provided by Mr. Nigel Malthus.
Page 36—"Venus" used courtesy of the Naturhistorisches Museum, Vienna, Austria

Cover and interior designed by Lise Rousseau.

ISBN 0-9706204-0-3

Contents

Dedicated to the Team —

Lisanne, Cathy, Lindsay, Lise, Ben, Eric, Rhonda, Marci,
Alison, Lori, Michel, Teresa, Ellen, Annette, Susan, Matt,
Marcie, Erin, Ken, Kristin, Pam, Amy, Wendy, Julia, & RachAel

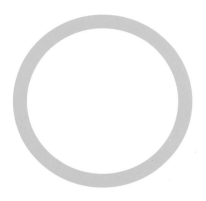

Introduction

Planet Awakening is based on an original booklet written in 1994 entitled, *Faith, Justice and a Healthy World*. *Faith, Justice and a Healthy World*, funded by the Pew Global Stewardship Initiative, was published prior to the United Nations International Conference on Population and Development (ICPD), and devoted to furthering the dialogue among people of faith on the complex issue of population and environment.

    Planet Awakening has been written with funding from the David and Lucile Packard Foundation under its new PLANet project, an effort to increase public awareness about international family planning. This new document profits from *Faith, Justice and a Healthy World's* years of use at the local and national level, as well as the author's thought, writing and studies of values and belief systems in the intervening period. The aim of this publication is to first provide a basic primer on population—especially as it relates to the environment. The issues of humans' relationship to Earth, its non-human creatures and other members of the human family are an essential element of the story. For this reason we begin our discussion with creation.

    Following creation, the complexity of human population as we enter a new millennium makes a fitting second section to the book. Since the original publication, the world reached six billion people. The population growth projections for the future underline the challenges ahead. Our quality of life with six billion human inhabitants will be altered greatly with a population double that size.

A third section reviews the various belief systems on the subject of stewardship and the environment, with some connection to human population growth. This section was co-written with RachAel Ahrens, who took on the demanding task of researching the views of different religions on ecology, population and women. Since there are numerous Christian perspectives, we have attempted to collate the published positions of Christian denominations on these issues as well. For those we have left out, please excuse us.

The fourth section deals with many of the issues related to population which provoke controversy and prevent consensus building. The issues selected are based on our own experience in dealing with citizen groups and policy makers and are by no means comprehensive.

The fifth section is a resource list for those who would like to read additional material related to the subject area. We have tried to document our sources and also accumulate as many resources as possible to guide those who would like to further their own quest for information, knowledge and understanding.

Finally, a new addition to the original document is a small selection of sermons, prayers, and meditations that can be used in designing a celebration, ritual or memorial. We are grateful to those who were willing to contribute a piece to this section and hope that as you use this document you will share your ideas and experiences with us.

You will note that the outside margins on each page have been enlarged, specifically for your use. As you read this book and reflect on the various issues, thoughts and theories presented here, please use this space to record your own thoughts, doodles, questions, comments, etc.

We consider this publication a "living" document. Changes will be made as we receive feedback from users suggesting better ways to frame the issues. We would also like to expand our network of people concerned about finding solutions. Therefore, users are encouraged to be part of an ongoing dialogue by writing to us at the address in the appendix, visiting the website at www.audubonpopulation.org, and attending workshops on *Planet Awakening*.

We are deeply appreciative for the input on this revision that has been received from numerous Audubon population and environment leaders. Feedback from users helped us to refine many of the areas of discussion. Especially helpful have been comments provided by Dr. Howard Clinebell and the Reverend Dr. Gary Gunderson, co-workshop leaders on the religious outreach workshops under the PLANet project. In addition to RachAel Ahren's research, we appreciate input from Dr. Jo Sanzgiri, Dennis Phillips, Kenneth Strom and Lise Rousseau. Finally, we are greatly appreciative of the support from the Population Program staff of the David and Lucile Packard Foundation.

Please note: The icons that you will find illustrating each chapter and page are a graphical representation of the development of the icon for the "origin of the universe," utilizing ever more complex "seed of life" or "seed of the universe" spirals.

In the Beginning...

In the Beginning...

...there was only darkness everywhere—darkness and water. And the darkness gathered thick in places, crowding and then separating, crowding and separating...I make the world and lo, the world is finished. Thus I make the world, and lo! The world is finished.

Pima Indian Creation Story
(Campbell and Moyers 1988)

In the Beginning...

...there was only the great self reflected in the form of a person. Reflecting, it found nothing but itself. Then its first word was, "This am I." Then he realized, I indeed, I am this creation, for I have poured it forth from myself. In that way he became this creation. Verily, he who knows this becomes in this creation a creator.

Hindu Upanishads Creation Story, 8th Century B.C.

In the Beginning...

...the world was slush, for the waters and the mud were all stirred together. There was no sound, no birds in the air, no living things. The Creator made a little wagtail and commanded him to produce the Earth. The bird flew down over the black waters and the dismal swamp, but he did not know what to do or how to begin. He splashed and stomped and beat the slush with his tail. Finally a few dry places appeared—the islands of Ainu. The Ainu word for earth is moshiri, floating land, and the wagtail is sacred.

Ainu Creation Myth
(Sproul 1991)

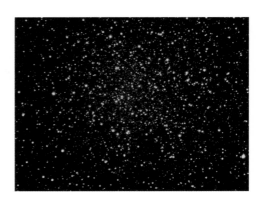

In the Beginning...

...God created heaven and earth, light and dark, waters, land, trees and plants. God also made fish, birds, and all the wild creatures on Earth. And God saw that it was good. God then wanted to create humans. God wanted humans to be a part of nature and so he asked each of the animals to help him plan. Each animal thought of the gift it would give to Man and Woman. "Make them brave," said the tiger. "Make them gentle," said the lamb. The chimpanzee chattered, "Let them always be curious." And the nightingale sang, "Give them voices that sing." "Good hearing," said the owl. "Good vision," said the hawk. "Playfulness," laughed the dolphin. The moon spoke. "Give them guidance." The sun shone. "Give them warmth." The stars sparkled. "Give them wonder." The trees stood tall. "Give them strength." Then God said that Woman and Man would have dominion over every living thing that creeps upon the Earth. The animals fled. "What will become of us?" God calmed them by saying, "I am creating Woman and Man in my own image and they shall be my partners in caring for you and all the world. In addition to your gifts, I will give them kindness and love. I will show them how to understand and reason so they can choose the right thing to do." The animals were afraid no longer. God created Woman and Man and nature lived in humankind. And God saw that it was good.

Jewish creation story
(Swartz 1998)

In the Beginning...

...when God created the heavens and the earth, the earth was a formless wasteland, and darkness covered the abyss, while a mighty wind swept over the waters. Then God said, "Let there be light," and there was light.

Genesis 1:1-3
(The Catholic Study Bible
1990)

Creation and Cosmology

From their beginnings, each faith has held a sacred story about the creation of life and all creatures of it. We may call the story a cosmology. All creation stories speak of the separation of dark and light, of earth and water. They also speak of the care given to seeding Earth and bringing plants and animals into life. And then they speak of humanity, one being who becomes separated into two.

There are often stories of a mountain, and others of a tree. Each story is filled with the symbolic significance that carries archetypal messages to the teachings about an omniscient Creator and the life that comes from the effort of creativity. The glory of creation is sung in praise of the miracle that is life. Even the minutest presence of life mirrors the face of its Creator. For this reason the idea of celebrating birds, animals, mountains, lakes, grass and even insects permeates the most wondrous of prose and poetry.

There are singular moments of magic and mysticism that occur in the most sacred depths of one's being. They may appear in the busiest minutes of a day through an epiphany or in a dreamlike state in the darkest hours of the night. Sometimes revelations come from walking in the woods, watching a bird nest in the trees, or following a trail of ants. The great Sufi mystic, Rumi, filled his poetry and prose with attention to these natural events.

> *Birdsong brings relief*
> *to my longing.*
>
> *I am just as ecstatic as they are,*
> *but with nothing to say!*
>
> *Please, universal soul, practice*
> *some song, or something, through me!*

And

> *Birds make great sky-circles*
> *of their freedom.*
>
> *How do they learn it?*
>
> *They fall, and falling,*
> *they're given wings.*

(Barks 1995, 243)

These moments of quiet are rare gifts. But Rumi's words teach us to fly with the birds. It is a time of letting go and being one with the rest of creation. The celebration of creation is one of the most fundamental values of environmentalism. Without the awesome marvel of the miracle of nature, we are left with the sterility of a closed, drab world, ungraced by diversity and surprise.

The fact that humans exist at all is a cause for celebration, and part of the wonder of the unveiling of the Big Bang, or as ecological theologians refer to it, the seed event. Brian Swimme, physicist and author, says that our principal task as humans is to live in the universe (Swimme 1996). What is the meaning of humans in this story of the unfolding of the universe?

The great Catholic scholar, Thomas Berry, speaks of whether humans play a unique role in nature's evolution. It is truly an environmentalist's best explanation for why diversity is important. Each piece of creation holds its own place, makes its own contribution, and provides something that no other piece can. Thus order is sustained because every piece of the puzzle is in place. Birds are the best flyers; fish are the best swimmers. Humans are the best thinkers (Stetson and Morrell 1999). The answer to how we best use our minds to reflect on the purpose and intent of humans in creation—whether caretaker, user or problem-solver—will be dealt with later in this essay.

The question is: What is the meaning of each individual life in the midst of this awesome creation? And what happens when the sheer numbers of lives begin to overwhelm that same creation which supports all life?

> *And after a long,*
> *lonesome and scary time*
> *the people listened*
> *and began to hear*
>
> *And to see God in one another*
> *and in the beauty of all the Earth.*
> (Wood 1992)

The hope is that people are beginning to listen to the Earth and to the various species of life, which speak in different ways. The wisdom of nature always has been around humanity, but not always heard, seen or interpreted. Today humans are threatening the ability to maintain the web of life of which they are a part. This threat is leading to a resurgence of interest in looking at the spiritual connections between humans and the Earth, and the responsibilities of all inhabitants to live in harmony with each other and with nature.

Our challenge is to evaluate our ethical system, which takes the best of religious beliefs and gives new guidance to people worldwide about how they can improve their lives and honor the planet, which is their home. We are called to reassess our system of values, regardless of our religious affiliation. A first step in this direction took place in 1986 when the World Wildlife Fund International brought together leaders from Hinduism, Buddhism, Judaism, Christianity, and Islam to discuss their vision of nature. This meeting in Assisi, Italy, resulted in a series of declarations regarding human conduct and responsibilities, and began the process of synthesis on the issues of faith and ecology.

That same year, a workshop at the Conference on Conservation and Development in Ottawa, Canada, resulted in an assessment of the ethical principles raised in the World Conservation Strategy by the concept of sustainable development. Many of those principles will be discussed later. The discussion of these principles by the Ethics Working Group of the International Union for the Conservation of Nature provided the basis for the book *Ethics and Development.*

However, for all of this intense work on ethics and the environment, the critical fact of human population growth was largely overlooked. Population as a subject has controversies; yet, the issues related to environment and sustainable development cannot be dealt with if population numbers and behavior are not a part of the considerations.

Further, most of the challenges related to population growth directly or indirectly relate to the fundamental issues of women's rights, education, employment and health. The fertility of women is directly related to the fertility of Earth, both of which are looked upon by some as spigots that can be controlled and manipulated. The rise of ecofeminism recognizes that relationship and the feminine creativity of not only Earth, but also all humankind. The same forces that do not view the human body as sacred also do not regard the sacredness of Earth.

Our calling as theologians, pastors, spiritual directors

and lay persons is to reframe the dialogue around population growth and consumption, and bring to bear ethical and spiritual principles, without pretending to have answers to these complex sets of problems. It is our hope that people can begin to think, discuss, and debate the essential linkages between people and people, and people and nature.

Saving this planet for all forms of life will require partnerships between and among all nations; and it is our responsibility, in the United States, to do much more than has been done before to redefine how we share the Earth with other peoples and wildlife. (Waak and Strom 1992, 13)

Population: How Do We Define the Problem?

Marching into a new millennium we are faced with escalating conflicts between activities which support the economic enterprises of humans and those that promote a healthy natural world. For example, the number of species threatened with extinction is reaching an all time high, and the situation promises to become much worse in the coming years (Myers et al. 2000, 853). Wildlife habitats are converted to shopping centers, housing divisions, croplands or cattle ranges.

All species ultimately are dependent on the same resource base. A world with wildlife is a world that is healthy for people. A world devoid of natural wonders is not only an aesthetic and spiritual loss; it is also a portent of a world unable to support a healthy humanity. In recent years, the rise in human population, and the resulting changes in the Earth, have brought a new realization that the natural world may be disappearing at an alarming rate.

Thomas R. Malthus 1766-1834

Population Theory: Malthus Revisited

In 1798, Thomas Robert Malthus, an English clergyman and economist, published a treatise entitled, *Essay on the Principle of Population.* His basic hypothesis was that human population, if unchecked, would increase geometrically while food production could increase only arithmetically. Human population would outstrip the

Earth's capacity for food production. Starvation, disease, and war would eventually lead to a human population crash similar to the biological decline of other species.

The theory of Malthusian overpopulation became the basis for continued speculation on the impact of human population increase, and the center of debate among such noted figures as Karl Marx, U.S. land reformer Henry George, and Danish economist Esther Boserup. In the late 1960s, modern perspectives were brought into play with the publication of Paul Ehrlich's *The Population Bomb*. Dr. Ehrlich predicted massive famines for the period from 1970 to 1985.

In 1972, U.S. economists Dennis and Donella Meadows produced *The Limits to Growth*, an important study, which added to the debate. A computer model projected trends in population, resource use, food production and a number of other areas. The research of Meadows and others tested various scenarios and came to the conclusion that population growth and use of resources always would exceed the long-term carrying capacity of the Earth. One scenario of *The Limits to Growth* study was favorable: It was based on reduction in resource use, adoption of solar energy, conservation of soil, institution of recycling, conversion from manufacturing to service industries, and stabilization of global population at less than four billion.

In 1980, the Council on Environmental Quality and the U.S. Department of State issued *The Global 2000 Report to the President*. The study was the result of a three-year effort by major government agencies to project the impacts of continued population growth on a wide range of resources. Critics of the report, like U.S. economist Julian Simon, countered with a hypothesis that population growth creates a large pool of workers and provides for the possibility of additional geniuses to develop technological innovations to overcome potential resource shortages. What could not be taken care of by technology, these critics claimed, could be resolved by the manipulation of a free-market economy.

In 1992, an updated work was produced by Donella Meadows and her associates entitled, *Beyond the Limits: Confronting Global Collapse, Envisioning a Sustainable Future*. The new projections indicated that the world was already over some limits, and current trends would present the global community with economic and environmental crises during the 21st century. Clearly the need for changes in some of the variables, like population, resources use, food production and pollution, were needed (Miller, 269).

While the massive mortality of humans from starvation has not come to pass worldwide, many countries are experiencing cycles of famine, environmental decline and death. In the past fifty years, ecologists have pointed to signs of environmental degradation, which is strongly correlated with rapid human population growth. The global community also has recognized that when the environment is considered, the unsustainable consumption of resources is an important factor in combination with population size. A model developed by Paul Ehrlich and John Holdren is called IPAT. The number of people (P) times the number of units of resources used per person, or affluence (A), times the environmental degradation and pollution per unit of resource use, or technology (T) equals the environmental impact of a given population (I) (Miller, 21).

$$I = P \times A \times T$$

— Paul Ehrlich and John Holdren

Human population is transforming the natural ecosystems. Among the general public, individuals asked about population often respond by nodding and mentioning images of crowded streets in Calcutta or starvation in Ethiopia. However, in our aging population a growing number of people have actually seen the landscape changed by human activity during their lifetime. According to scientific studies, it is estimated that between 39% and 50% of the land on our planet has been transformed or degraded by humans (Vitousek et al. 1997, 495).

However, the word population is only lately linked closely with these environmental changes. More often, population is associated with growth and development of economies; sales markets for baby food, diapers, and other consumer products; pro-choice and anti-abortion confrontations before the U.S. Supreme Court. Many people in the United States remember *Soylent Green*, the science fiction movie that takes place in a polluted, overpopulated New York City. Today, North Americans commonly recognize local population issues like the disappearance of open space, crowded highways and streets, and advancing sprawl.

Population, first and foremost, is about numbers of people and the dynamics of their growth. It is the numbers that form the beginning of the story.

The Numbers

Almost all creation stories begin with a couple living in harmony with the world. According to archeological and anthropological discoveries, the first humans lived one to two million years ago in Africa and probably were never greater in number than 125,000. Disease, accidents, wars, and scarce food supplies limited population growth. Hunter-gatherer societies' mobility resulted in low impact on the resources and low fertility because of the need to move with their children.

Agriculture changed all of that. Control over food supply expanded the ability to feed more people. It also resulted in improved diets. The transition to agriculture resulted in higher density populations and establishment of structured communities. By the beginning of the modern era, the global human community numbered around 170 million (Harrison 1992, 8). The subsequent growth of human population fluctuated with disease, famine and war. For example, the Black Death, or bubonic plague, raged through human settlements beginning in 1346. From 1346-50, some communities were totally extinguished. In Europe alone one third of the total population died (McNeill 1977, 147-148).

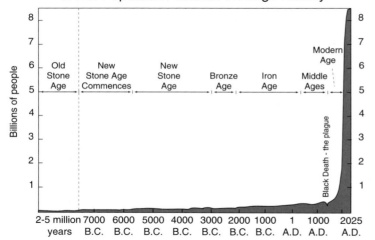

World Population Growth Through History

Source: Population Reference Bureau

By the time of Columbus' voyages to the New World, the population of the Earth numbered 500 million. Less than 300 years later, at American Independence, the number of Earth's human inhabitants reached 1 billion.

It took more than a century, to 1930, to go from 1 billion to 2 billion people. By 1960, just 30 years later, the planet had added its third billion. It took only half that time, 15 years, to grow to 4 billion, and 12 years to grow from 4 to 5 billion. Adding the 6th billion took 13 years, signifying the beginning of a decline in population growth rates.

Current projections for the year 2025 predict a world population of between 8 and 10 billion. The less developed countries will make up 7 to 9 billion of that total. More than three-quarters of the global population growth is occurring in those countries. Even though growth rates are slowing, the human population could rise to 14 billion before stabilizing.

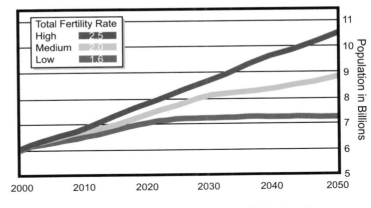

As former Vice President Al Gore noted, the world population will more than double, perhaps even triple, during his lifetime (Gore 1993, 5). This phenomenon, watching human population double or triple during one's lifetime, is unparalleled in history.

Total Fertility Rate is the average number of children a woman will have during her lifetime conforming to the age-specific fertility rates of a given year.

Source: United Nations, *World Population Prospects: The 1998 Revision*

Carrying Capacity

Most biological systems have limits. *Carrying capacity is the maximum number of organisms an environment—local, regional, or global—can support over a specified period of time* (Miller 2000, 5). The idea of carrying capacity can easily be demonstrated through theories of wildlife populations. An animal population will continue to grow within a certain area until the habitat can no longer support all the individuals. Food will become scarce, and there will be fierce competition for territory. Many animals will either migrate or die. This is nature's way of controlling population growth in relationship to the ability of an environment to sustain that population.

Humans have defied the traditional limits of biological carrying capacity through technology and the substitution of one resource for another. However, healthy human populations can survive over time only within the parameters of ecological carrying capacity. Only so much sulfur dioxide can be pumped into the atmosphere before it precipitates to the earth as acid rain. Lake ecosystems, normally buffered by waste-filtering microbes, can be overwhelmed and transformed into cesspools if sewage and toxins are continually dumped. Since human beings consume resources, and since human activity has an impact upon the natural environment, it follows that the inherent limitations of resources force a corresponding limit to the number of people who depend on them. Beyond these limitations, humans begin to deplete nonrenewable resources, or to convert renewable resources into nonrenewable ones (LeBlanc 1992).

Scientists continue to debate the question of the ultimate carrying capacity of the Earth for humans. Conversion to grain diets, redistribution of wealth, and use of all arable land are some of the measures we could take to extend the Earth's ability to accommodate more and more people. Perhaps the most telling commentary comes from Dr. Carl Djerassi of Stanford University. When asked some years ago what the carrying capacity of the Earth for humans might be, he responded:

> "That depends on what you think about the quality of life. If you mean standing up and having one meal a day, the number is enormous.
>
> If you're talking about the way we live now—which means misery for half the people in the world, a so-so life for a few others, and an attractive life for a few hundred million—than I think we've already exceeded the maximum" (Foreign Assistance Action Project 1988).

Cultures have gone into demise as a result of inability to live within the carrying capacity of their land base. The Anasazi Indians of the Southwestern United States and the Maya civilization of Central America are two examples of cultures which many archeologists believe declined or disappeared as a result of overpopulation and natural resource degradation. Other theorists point to expanded urbanization and consumerism as a cause of the decline and crash of Roman civilization.

The dramatic change in the human population growth rate is largely the result of new and laudable medical technologies, which have cured and prevented disease, and increased the life expectancy of millions of people. With modern technology and new genetic plant stock, the world has been able to feed itself, even though food is often unevenly distributed. The result is that the Earth's human population is expanding at an explosive rate in one part of the world, and human consumption is eating up the natural resources in another.

Demographic Transition

The industrial revolution in Europe is often pointed to as an example of the classic pattern of "demographic transition," and of the capacity for stabilizing population growth. In the beginning of the transition, birth and death rates were high. As death rates dropped with the arrival of better sanitation and higher standards of living, birth rates initially remained high. Then economic and social improvements combined with lowered infant mortality rates led to a desire for fewer children and a decline in the birth rate. The result was an equalization of birth and death rates to a level of stability in some countries, and even to fewer births than deaths in many European countries.

This European model often has been cited as evidence that economic development can in and of itself solve the population growth problem. Paul Kennedy in his book, *Preparing for the Twenty-First Century*, points out that massive out-migration of population was also a key factor in England's economic and demographic transformation (1993). However, the recent pattern of demographic transition has been different in less developed countries. In the poorer countries, the drop in birth rates has not occurred as quickly as the fall in death rates. The result is continued population growth, often too rapid for the economies of those countries to adjust to the sheer number of people.

Despite *falling* growth rates, the world's population continues to grow. This is not because women are having more and more children. In fact, the average number of children born to women of reproductive age in developing countries (excluding China) has declined from 6.2

Population pyramids from Kenya, the U.S. and Italy demonstrate a rapidly growing and young population (Kenya), a slower growing population (U.S.) and a shrinking population (Italy).

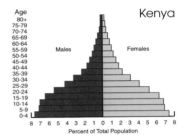

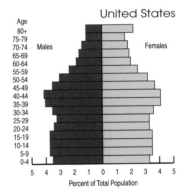

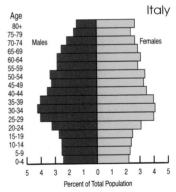

Source: U.S. Census Bureau

children per woman in the early 1960s to 3.7 children today. But there are more women of childbearing age than ever before, resulting in a "demographic momentum." This momentum means that world population will continue to grow as young people reach reproductive age.

For example, recent surveys of Kenya indicate the annual rate of natural increase has dropped from 4.1% to 2.1%. Yet Kenya's population is projected to rise from 30 million to 34 million by 2025. The life expectancy for a Kenyan man is 48 years and he could see his country's population double—or more—during his lifetime. Pakistan, with 151 million people in 2000, could double its population in 25 years if birth and death rates remain constant. Pakistan is projected to reach 227 million by 2025. Guatemala, with a current population of 12.7 million people, is projected to reach a level of 22.3 million by 2025. All of these scenarios are based on projections from the Population Reference Bureau and factor in births, deaths and number of women of reproductive age. The longest life expectancy for females in the developing world (sixty-seven years) is in Guatemala.

Definition of Overpopulation

Measuring population represents more than counting people or animals. It includes evaluating the quality of life for individuals and their consumption of resources. Overpopulation exists when the numbers of people and/or their consumption patterns degrade or destroy the natural resources on which all life depends.

In 1999, global population reached six billion. Eighty percent of the global population live in what can be called "less developed" countries. The 1999 per capita GNP for these countries, including China, was US$1,260. Latin American countries were a little better off with per capita GNP of US$3,880. But in African countries, the per capita GNP averaged US$670. The average population doubling time (the number of years in which a population would double assuming a constant rate of natural increase) was 29 years in Africa and 39 years in Latin America, an improvement over previous years. When Asian countries are added, the percentage of countries with developing economies rises to over 75% and the average per capita GNP in Asia is slightly above US$2,000 (PRB 2000).

By contrast, the most recent 2000 World Population Data Sheet shows the United States' population doubling time through natural increase as 120 years and the per capita GNP as $29,240. U.S. population is growing faster than the natural rate of increase because of migration from other countries. Part of the reason for this migration is the economic disparity between "less developed" and "more developed" countries.

Achieving and guaranteeing a better life in material terms for citizens of industrialized nations has major consequences for the global ecosystem. The effects of population growth on the human environment in the United States are most evident in crowding, congestion, and pollution. While many people in industrialized countries tend not to use the term "overpopulation" in describing their situations, they can feel the effects of poorly planned communities, traffic jams, overcrowded recreation areas, poor air quality, and water shortages. Those who live in Tucson, Arizona, or Naples, Florida, have witnessed dramatic changes in the past two decades, particularly with regard to available water resources. Inhabitants of the densely populated bay areas of San Francisco, Delaware or the Chesapeake are experiencing major degradation of their fisheries and coastal marine life. Expanding urban sprawl is contributing to the loss of wildlife species and open space in almost every major city in the United States.

The growth issues in Europe and Japan are as severe as those described in the United States. Loss of forests, polluted rivers, industrial waste, and crowded living space have forced an urgent look at traditional economic assumptions and practices. What we have long considered "progress" is leading to detrimental or dangerous conditions for millions of people.

In industrialized countries, imbalances occur when groups of people seek a standard of living that cannot be

> The impact of any given population is affected by the size of its "appetite."

Population in millions

Legend:
- Population Adjusted for Consumption
- Actual Population

Categories: China, India, Soviet Union, United States, Canada

Source: The Earth Council, 1994

sustained without degrading the natural resource base, and when modes of production pose a physical threat to the environment and to people. On average, Americans consume more resources and produce more waste per person than any other country (President's Council on Sustainable Development 1996). Industrial countries consume from 75 to 86 % of the world's supply of aluminum, chemicals, paper, iron and steel, timber and energy (Durning 1992, 50). The result is tremendous pressure on both the domestic and global environment. The signs of overconsumption can be seen in declining air and water quality, the loss of topsoil and forests, the degradation of river and coastal systems, and the loss of wildlife and wetlands.

Seventy-five percent of the United States population lives in urban centers. As the centers grow, they experience problems with sanitation and with access to basic human services. Today, in modern cities of the most industrialized countries, the shift of populations to urban settings has contributed to the growing numbers of homeless people living on the margin of economic survival.

Urban growth in several parts of the United States exacerbates already existing problems. The states of California, Arizona, Texas, and Florida continue to grow, as political, economic, and environmental refugees enter, legally and illegally, in search of a better life. However, in-migration from other parts of the United States is also a factor in the growth of these states, particularly as an increasingly older U.S. population reaches retirement age and looks for a hospitable climate and lifestyle. The "Interior West," composed of the states of Montana, Idaho, Wyoming, Colorado, Utah, Nevada, Arizona and New Mexico, received more people between 1990 and 1994 than moved away from it (Reibsame et al. 1997, 95).

As in the "Interior West," population growth can be a function of in-migration.

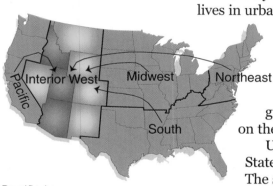

Pacific to
Interior West 386,017

Midwest to
Interior West 90,197

Northeast to
Interior West 118,702

South to
Interior West 34,221

Source: Center of the American West, 1998

Population Growth and Biological Diversity

In order to have food, a home, and support for their families, people clear land, farm it, and build on it, radically altering its vegetation and wildlife. In developing countries, the number of people without access to arable land has surged. Families are clearing parks, wildlife preserves, and tropical forests in their search for livelihoods.

In countries like the United States, wetlands are being sacrificed to more paved roads, homes, apartment houses, schools, hospitals, and recreation facilities. Agricultural, industrial, and urban expansion has depleted water sources, polluted air and water, and damaged unique ecosystems. Wildlife is drowned, displaced, starved, run over, and outcompeted by human needs.

There is a limit to our planet's resources. New homes, industries, and farms displace natural ecosystems and, in extreme cases, destroy the life-support systems those ecosystems once provided, resulting in starvation and extinction of native wildlife. This global problem presents major challenges for environmental, political, and social adaptation.

The Global Nature of the Problem

Population growth, and the associated use of resources by growing numbers of people, is indeed a global challenge. The evidence of transboundary issues fills the news media every day. The United States and Canada have been struggling over acid rain regulations for years. Environmental considerations have framed much of the North American Free Trade Agreement (NAFTA) between the U.S., Canada and Mexico. Erosion by the major river system in India starts in Nepal, Bhutan, and China. Deforestation in Nepal provokes flooding in Bangladesh. Migration across borders in Africa contributes to soil erosion and exhaustion of fertile land.

The burning of the Amazon and other rain forests, along with the burning of fossil fuel for cars and industry in the U.S. and other industrialized countries, produces some 80% of the carbon dioxide emissions that are changing the global climate. At the same time, the old growth forests of the U.S. Pacific Northwest are disappearing at an alarming rate primarily to supply markets in Japan.

The trend toward urbanization is a global pattern. The growth of mega-cities around the world has occurred in a short four decades. In 1950, New York was the only city with a population over 10 million. By 2000, the top five cities in the world were Tokyo, Japan, with 28 million; Mexico City, Mexico with 18.1 million; Bombay, India with 18 million; Sao Paulo, Brazil with 17.7 million; and New York, New York with 16.6 million. The real significant projection is that the number of cities in developing countries with 10 million or more citizens will increase from 10 to 22 in twenty years. The urban population will increase to more than 4 billion globally, while the rural population will basically remain the same (Population Reference Bureau Website 2000).

As cities grow, the need for energy expands. Today, the burgeoning human population demands potentially destructive levels of energy use. Emissions from the plants that generate electricity, and from vehicles and other fuel combustion, contaminate air, water, and soil. At the global level, these emissions are resulting in atmospheric change.

Major global problems like depletion of the ozone layer, loss of biological diversity, deforestation, soil erosion, desertification, and water pollution all are connected directly or indirectly to just one of millions of species living on this Earth—people. One of the most critical issues facing future human populations is often ignored: a need for twice as much fresh water in the coming decade as is needed today.

Population growth is highest and poverty at its most extreme in the tropical countries. Families are driven by poverty to find whatever ways they can to earn income, develop farmland for food, and find wood for energy use. Increasingly, slash-and-burn agriculture and firewood collection are destroying the richest habitats on Earth. With fewer trees to absorb precipitation, evaporation and water runoff increase. Soil and nutrients are lost; forest regeneration halts. Most of the species of tropical forests, once lost, are gone forever; they do not occur in second growth.

In addition to extirpating the forests' unique plants and wildlife, these human activities also guarantee that there will be even less food available for future generations. A drop in per capita food production in Africa and the Middle East in the past decade correlates to an increase in deforestation, desertification, and overpopulation.

The Earth's greatest biological diversity is found in tropical forests. Throughout the world, failure to protect biological diversity is becoming an overwhelming problem. Besides animal species, the wild plants form important gene pools for agriculture and medicine.

Deforestation is directly related to the loss of species and has a role to play in the potential for global climate change. It is only recently that research on atmospheric changes has documented the connections. The conclusion is that the powerfully devastating changes taking place in the global atmosphere are related to human population growth. While deforestation is a contributor to these changes, the growth of polluting industries and use of fossil fuel based vehicles make industrialized countries the source of over one-half of the greenhouse gases pumped into the atmosphere.

Measurements indicate that the Earth's temperature is going up. The culprit: a buildup of carbon dioxide in the atmosphere from the burning of fossil fuels and deforestation. The result is the trapping of heat in the atmosphere. Scientists now believe that methane, as well as chlorofluorocarbons, nitrous oxide and ozone, are implicated in this atmospheric change. And certainly the expanding hole in the ozone layer adds to the other changes taking place.

Carbon dioxide and methane analyzed from air trapped centuries ago in polar ice show that levels of carbon dioxide in the atmosphere rose by nearly 25% from the 1750s until today (McKibben 1989, 12). Methane levels have been rising in tandem with human population growth as a result of increased cattle production, agriculture, coal mining, and fossil fuel burning.

Who Benefits, Who Doesn't?

Today, more than one billion of the six billion people on Earth live in abject poverty. Dr. Nafis Sadik, former Executive Director of the United Nations Population Fund, asks: "Can the Earth meet even modest aspirations for the bottom billion, let alone those of the better-off and their descendants, without irreparable damage to its life-support systems?" Is there not a close connection between overuse and destruction of the natural world and a failure to maintain a reasonable standard of living for human inhabitants?

The failure to provide women with options for their roles in society has only exacerbated the situation. When women bear large numbers of children, they often sacrifice their basic rights to health, employment, education, and the opportunity to play a meaningful role in society. Surveys indicate that women around the world want the same things for their children: good health, education, jobs, adequate food, and housing. The challenge then is to provide women with the means to provide their children with a safe and healthy future.

Most governments and private health care organizations realize that multiple births and short intervals between births endanger the health of mother and child. There are success stories in family planning that include countries like Zimbabwe, Mexico, and Indonesia. In Thailand, innovative programs have combined family planning and health with community development and resource conservation.

However, the current world expenditures on the provision of reproductive health and family planning services must be doubled in the next decade if the world community is to meet the demand for child spacing and fertility regulation. This level of services includes expenditures by donor governments, multilateral population groups, and national governments. The past quarter-century has brought major advances in services delivered: a concentration on identifying and meeting family needs, health and family planning care delivered at the village and community level, and training of local people to provide the care needed. Current programs are insufficient to respond to the burgeoning demands of women and families. Without services, education, and employment, women are still caught in an endless cycle of poverty.

Overall, most people in developed nations enjoy the benefits of wealth sufficient to support comfortable lifestyles, while less developed nations bear the cost in depletion of resources. An American consumes many times the natural resources that a poor Kenyan uses. The impact of U.S. consumption is felt locally and globally. Production, use, and disposal of plastics, fertilizers, and chemicals alter habitats and pollute the environment. Rapid development overruns unique ecosystems. It becomes increasingly difficult to provide social services. Traffic jams, urban stress, toxic waste scares, contaminated food and water and the impossibility of finding a parking place are commonplace in everyday life.

Solutions

Unfortunately, the world wants a quick answer to complex questions. A long debate over the cause and effect of environmental degradation has pitted good scientists and lay people against each other and prevented the collaborative work necessary for the promotion of hope and the discovery of solutions. In particular, women espousing justice for other women have found themselves arguing over whether population growth has any relationship to environmental quality. Many women's rights advocates fear that by acknowledging the relationship between population growth and environment they will "blame" poor women for environmental degradation.

There is no *one* cause and effect. It is clear that rapid population growth, economic instability, and a degraded environment are part of a cycle. The poorest countries are caught in a cycle of poverty, rapid population growth, and environmental degradation. The richer countries have their own cycle of "throw away" ethics and overconsumption, population density, and environmental degradation. Neither of these two situations has provided an answer for their local dilemma, much less to the global issues in which all humans, rich or poor, are interdependent.

Finding solutions requires a commitment to live as a global society. More and more, developing countries realize that a combination of population stabilization, equitable economic development, and conservation of natural resources will make the difference that allows for short- and long-term survival. The need is for encouragement, plus financial and technical assistance for policies and practices that reduce human impacts on ecological resources. In developed countries the formula is only slightly different. The answers lie in growth management of cities and communities, reassessment of economic values and systems, and conservation for long-term sustainable use. Priorities must include a long-range vision, changes in lifestyles, commitment to an Earth ethic and organized action.

In 1994, the United Nations (UN) International Conference on Population and Development (ICPD) was held in Cairo, Egypt. This landmark conference ended with more consensus than any previous population conference. By defining a new relationship between governments and private citizens, the Programme of Action for 180 countries moved beyond a demographic focus to a global concept of sustainable development, including resource consumption and environmental management (ICPD 1994). More importantly, the gathering in Cairo put a woman's face on population by emphasizing the need for women's education, comprehensive reproductive health care, reproductive rights, and female political and social empowerment (Waak 1995).

For several years, a growing international community of citizens, along with their governments, has advocated the complex of priorities known by the term "sustainable development." The concept of sustainable development embraces four major points:

◆ First, economic development is linked to environmental sustainability. For example, cash crops for export may increase economic returns, but if they leach the soil, degrade the land, and otherwise contribute to loss of the natural resource base, they are not sustainable.

◆ Second, sustainable development recognizes a growing global interdependence and promotes an integrated approach to "interlocking crises." For example, the interrelationships between population growth and consumption; agriculture and food

"Poverty has a female face."

— Dr. Noeleen Heyzer, *Ethics for a Small Planet,* Daniel C. Maguire security; environment and natural resource management; technology and industry; and the literacy and status of women must all be viewed together. None of these sectors operate alone.

♦ Third, sustainable development is more concerned with long-term rather than with short-term development goals. The consequences of policies and programs have to be factored out over future decades. We must begin to plan for fifty years or more rather than one.

♦ And fourth, sustainable development recognizes a generational responsibility. In the words of the World Commission on Environment and Development, in *Our Common Future*, "Sustainable development is development that meets the needs of the present without compromising the ability of future generations to meet their own needs."

An important part of sustainable development will be a commitment on the part of individual countries to stabilizing population growth while providing for the basic needs of their people. Those countries that have been successful in moving toward this goal indicate that the following factors are important in making programs and policies work:

1) A partnership between government and nongovernmental organizations (NGOs)

2) Participation by local people in the design and implementation of their own programs and services

3) A commitment to the five essential factors related to fertility decline: increased women's education; opportunities for women's employment; a rise in women's legal and social status; decrease in infant mortality; and access to women's reproductive health services including family planning. An additional essential ingredient is the education of men

4) A dedication of the necessary financial and human resources by both the rich and the poorer countries

These principles can apply to both developed and developing countries. For this reason, the United States has a special responsibility to look at its own population issues. With a population of 275 million people, the United States is the third largest country in the world. A

As a percentage of its GNP, U.S. spending for official development assistance is in last place among donor countries.

	% of GNP
Denmark	1.01
Norway	0.92
Sweden	0.86
Netherlands	0.79
France	0.56
Canada	0.38
Switzerland	0.35
Belgium	0.35
Australia	0.33
Germany	0.33
Finland	0.32
Austria	0.30
United Kingdom	0.29
Ireland	0.28
Portugal	0.28
Japan	0.26
Spain	0.25
New Zealand	0.23
Italy	0.21
United States	0.12

Source: Population Action International

baby born in the United States today will consume over his or her lifetime 30 times the resources that would be consumed by a baby born in India. Population and consumption combined make the United States one of the most overpopulated countries in the world.

In 1999, the world community once more looked at the global population situation through the lens of the Cairo document. The good news is that the rate of population growth is slowing. The bad news is that the total number of people living in poverty continues to grow. The good news is that less developed countries met their commitment to provide ¾ of the required resources to meet the needs of women, children and their families. The terrible news is that the donor countries have not contributed their full share. The United States, in fact, has failed to increase its funding since 1994 and currently only provides ⅓ of its funding commitment.

The solution to meeting the challenge of improving individual lives and decreasing population growth lies in making our voices heard on behalf of the voiceless. Population is the single most important environmental issue facing us, whether considered in terms of our numbers, where we choose to live, or what resources we use. A key to meeting this challenge lies in the embodiment of our values and belief systems through action, as well as a commitment to justice.

Ethics, Morality and Religion

While the religious community has begun to embrace the issues of the environment and of poverty, there has been great reluctance to deal with population issues. For many people of faith, poverty is identified as the fundamental issue for society. If we focus on poverty and ignore population growth, it is easier to avoid confrontation with the controversies surrounding population. Even reducing consumption of resources has found a home for itself within faith communities long before tackling population growth has.

Human life on this planet has looked continually for contact with "the divine." The enormous consequences of too many children and not enough food are only some of the distractions of staying alive—leaving little time for spiritual nourishment.

The reluctance of organized religion to deal with population is best understood by reviewing some of the major attitudes through time. The following is a brief overview and does not pretend to be comprehensive. We hope this summary will set the stage for continued discussion among people of faith who care deeply about life on this planet.

Ancient Traditional Religions

It is unclear at what point humans became conscious of a higher being. All existing records of historic societies indicate that elements in the natural world almost always were honored. Ancient myths are filled with stories of

"Our churches must lead the way and teach the seriousness of our ecological predicament and become involved in healing the earth."

— Bruce Babbit in the *Green Cross Newsletter*, May 1997

"Venus" of Willendorf
c. 24,000-22,000 B.C.E.
Naturhistorisches Museum,
Vienna

spirits in rivers, trees, rocks, and animals. These elements are illustrated in the cave paintings of Europe and Africa. Today, remnants of that reverence for nature are found in more traditional societies.

This connection with the Earth is best embodied in the term "Mother Earth." Ancient religions honored the Mother Goddess, an image of nurture, creativity and fertility that brought forth life. Early communities were matrifocal and communal, with strong emphasis on, and honor to, Earth as the source of life and death.

Women in these cultures have traditionally been portrayed as the healers and nurturers, and allied with the production of food, the caretakers of the agrarian society. Historically in these communities, women did not always want to have children, and practiced techniques to control fertility that included herbal contraceptives and abortifacients. Ancient stories tell of women so in tune with nature and their own bodies that they could prevent conception through meditation alone (Sjoo and Mor 1987, 388-9).

When women were in natural control of their own fertility, family size was always kept in reasonable balance with the needs of the group and the abundance of the environment. Because women valued the quality of life experienced by their children, they did what they could do to keep population in balance with the environment.

Indigenous people worshiped an array of spirits and still perform ceremonies and rituals to nature. In Africa, the divinity of all things is reflected in the early art of the Egyptians. Almost every tribal group today carries a deep mystical connection with Earth, animals and spirits. It is this "oneness" with the natural world that gives value, in the circle of life, to animals and the elements of nature.

The concept of Popular Traditional African Religion Everywhere (PTARE) is helpful in understanding this heritage. The wisdom of basic African spiritual practices is connected with the practical wisdom and knowledge of tribal people (Asante and Abarry 1996). The matriarchal and matrilineal aspects of African spirituality form a link between ancient worship of the Mother Goddess and the indigenous beliefs characteristic of the American Indian. The same principles of unity, elimination of chaos, elevation of peace, creation of harmony and balance exist in all these spiritual approaches.

Within the American Indian heritages, giving thanks to those aspects of nature which support and nurture life were passed from generation to generation. Chief Luther Standing Bear, a member of the Lakota who inhabited Nebraska and the Dakotas, echoes these traditions: "Kinship with all creatures of the earth, sky and water was a real and active principle. For the animal and bird world there existed a brotherly feeling that kept the Lakota safe among them, and so close did some of the Lakotas come to their feathered and furred friends that in true brotherhood they spoke a common tongue."

In these traditions, people emulated their brothers and sisters in the animal world. Population was kept in balance with what both the human and natural community could bear. However, disruption of tribal communities, mass extinctions of people, and forced movement off traditional lands often led to higher fertility.

"Humankind has not woven the web of life. We are but one thread within it. Whatever we do to the web, we do to ourselves. All things are bound together. All things connect."

— Chief Seattle

Guarding the Land

Native Americans such as the Hupa, Yurok, Karok, Shasta, Tolowa and Takelma made southwestern Oregon one of the world's most diverse cultural areas.

What often united these cultures was a belief in "supernatural guardians" that protected people and the land. More than 140 tribes in North America knew of "little people" or "dwarfs."

The Hupa, Karok, and Yurok believed in a bearded dwarf who provided just enough food so people would have enough to eat. But if the dwarf saw wasted food, he produced a famine. Similar was the Rock Old Woman, who punished selfish, greedy Takelma shamans, those who ignored the communal good. Some Tolowa and Shasta respected the power of privacy of "little people" and avoided areas where they were seen. As a result, such areas were given a chance to recover from resource use.

Nature guardians encouraged stable populations as well as frugal use of resources. Kwakiutl in Canada who had too many children believed their magic returned to the Wild Man. "Little people" known to five tribes were said to have started death or floods so people wouldn't overpopulate the Earth. This may be why the social ideal of the Hupa and Yurok was to have few children.

The belief in little people formed part of a broader Native American view that saw the world as alive and conscious. Actions by individuals had repercussions that reflected back on their community and their world, in part because the difference between humans and the rest of the world wasn't felt to be great. It wasn't nice to fool Mother Nature or her guardians; retribution could be a swift accident or a lingering drought.

This contrasts strikingly with western attitudes. Many in our culture feel we can do anything we want to nature without fear of punishment. Nature guardians don't limit our greed or selfishness. Nature has become an insignificant "other" for exploitation with which we no longer identify.

Concern about retribution may have helped keep resource use per person to less than 1/40th that of most modern Americans. Even today, many reservation people refuse to adopt highly consumptive lifestyles. They live simply so that others may simply live.

It may be that few cultures ever halted population growth, a rise that eventually drove groups into agriculture and increasing exploitation, along with attitudes that justify such use. But this can change if an awareness of the results of our actions, combined with a love of Nature, can replace "supernatural" controls on human impacts.

(With permission of Oregon Caves Underworld, the newsletter of the Crater Lake Natural History Association.)

Religion, Ecology, Women and Population

The transition in focus from biocentrism to anthropocentrism provides a vastly different approach to human responsibility to and for nature. Much of the discussion today in the modern Judeo-Christian tradition is over the meaning of one particular word in Genesis: *dominion*, as illustrated in the following scripture.

> *"God blessed them and God said to them, 'Be fruitful and multiply, and fill the earth and subdue it; and have dominion over the fish of the sea and over the birds of the air and over every living thing that moves upon the earth'."* Genesis 1:28 NRSV

The substantive word in this passage pertains to blessing. Obedience to the will of the Creator signified that state of blessing. Theologian Karen Armstrong points to disobedience leading to God's curse. She believes that the chief blessing was that of human fertility. "In an age when infant mortality was high and childbearing perilous, abundance of progeny was understandably prized." Today greed has led to "a selfish rape of the planet" and "childbearing and fertility have become a potential danger as we face a population explosion of fearful proportions" (Armstrong 1997, 31).

The whole question of dominion over the Earth is raising new questions. Does dominion refer to domination of humans over nature? Does dominion mean to practice stewardship and therefore imply a responsibility? Are we squandering our blessings of fertility, both that of humans and of Earth? Is the curse of Eden not our unwillingness to listen to Creation?

> "Even though we are unique in creation, there are absolute limits on human behavior and our choices on how we use God's creation."
>
> — *Keeping the Earth*

Judaism and Ecology

The Torah states, "In the beginning, God created Heaven and Earth." Jewish tradition has thought of Earth as a possession of God that can be enjoyed but must also be protected and kept by human beings. Because human beings are only tenants of God's creation, we have a responsibility to protect and serve Earth as a divine trust. "Bal tashchit," prohibition of wanton destruction (and which literally means, "do not destroy"), has often been

Ask the animals, and they will teach you, or the birds of the air, and they will tell you.

— Job 12:7

used as the basis for a Jewish environmental ethic (Chapman, Petersen, and Smith-Moran 2000, 137). The Sabbath also contains an important conservation element. In addition to resting the land every seven days, farmers are also directed to allow their farmland to lie fallow every seven years. Judaism recognizes that there are absolute limits to human behavior with regards to the environment.

Jewish ethic promotes simple, sustainable lifestyles and a balance of wealth and resources between every person. Because population growth and environmental damage are often attributed to an imbalanced distribution of wealth and health care and an unjust treatment of women, they are becoming a major priority in the Jewish community. By saying to Adam and Eve in the Garden of Eden, "Be fruitful and multiply," God did intend for humans to populate Earth. But what is often overlooked in this interpretation is that God also gave this commandment to animals and plants. Humans have filled the world with people as God wanted and now the moral duty to multiply does not apply. Responsible family planning then becomes a rational solution. Jews recognize that population growth contributes to poverty, human suffering, and unequal distribution of resources, as well as environmental damage. Jews also realize that our relationship to God is not a reflection of how many children we have, but rather of our relationships with and treatment of other human beings.

Christianity and Ecology

The patriarchal Christian church began a shift in focus away from the Earth and toward the sky or heaven, retaining the mother figure only through the Virgin Mary. The care of *humans* became central to existence in the rapidly urbanizing landscape, and the emphasis on the value of all creatures within the ecosystem lost its potency.

One noted religious leader said on Earth Day in 1990 that one should remember that the Earth was put here for humans, not the other way around (O'Conner 1990). There are, in fact, many views within the Christian religious community, including an emphasis on the words of Genesis, which point to God's pleasure with *all*

of creation. Within the Christian church, there exist numerous examples of care for the broader ecosystem and an understanding of the interdependence between humans and other species of life. St. Francis of Assisi, patron saint of animals and ecology, is an obvious example of this view of humans' relationship with the environment.

The views of Christians are often very diverse, making it difficult to give a "Christian" response to the population crisis. The Roman Catholic Pope is one of Christianity's voices on issues such as women's empowerment, family planning, and population issues. A single voice often does not give a response broad enough to cover all Christian opinions, and later in this document we have tried to include a synopsis of some major Christian denominations' approaches to these issues. Nevertheless, Christians can agree that humans have been acting carelessly with God's creation, and action must be taken to make human presence on Earth less ecologically devastating.

Christians believe that humans, plants, and animals are God's creation and are therefore precious. The Bible has many verses that explicitly give instruction on how to care for the Earth and its inhabitants. "The Lord God took man and put him in the Garden of Eden to till it and keep it" (Genesis 2:15). This line of the Bible is interpreted by many Christians as permission to use Earth's resources, but it also implies responsibility for keeping Earth beautiful and being mindful of one's impact on the planet.

Population issues can be controversial in Christianity. Coercive forms of birth control are unacceptable, although many Christians support voluntary family planning as a way to better provide for existing children and decrease the burden of population on the environment. Many congregations are "greening" their churches and teaching the importance of a healthy creation. Although the Vatican opposes artificial birth control, many Christian families find that spacing or delaying children is better for the health of the family as well as the environment. Many Christians and individual clergy members are taking a stand to ensure women's reproductive rights issues are addressed by their churches. Promoting women's reproductive rights, greening the

Excerpts from the Canticle of Brother Sun and Sister Moon of St. Francis of Assisi:

Praised be You my Lord with all Your creatures, especially Sir Brother Sun, Who is the day through whom You give us light. And he is beautiful and radiant with great splendour, Of You Most High, he bears the likeness.

Praised be You, my Lord, through Sister Moon and the stars, In the heavens you have made them bright, precious and fair.

Praised be You, my Lord, through Brothers Wind and Air, And fair and stormy, all weather's moods, by which You cherish all that You have made.

Praised be You my Lord through Sister Water, So useful, humble, precious and pure.

Praised be You my Lord through Brother Fire, through whom You light the night and he is beautiful and playful and robust and strong.

Praised be You my Lord through our Sister, Mother Earth who sustains and governs us, producing varied fruits with coloured flowers and herbs.

church, and teaching the importance of creation care are some of the first steps being taken to ensure a sustainable population and a healthy Earth.

To say that Christian attitudes toward women, population and the environment form a seamless approach denies the place that each denomination has reached in their deliberations on these subjects. The following is our best attempt at summarizing the statements of some of the Christian denominations.

The Baptist Church and Ecology

Baptists in the United States stand divided on many issues concerning population, women, and the environment. For example, the American Baptist Convention and the Southern Baptist Convention have different, sometimes conflicting, views on these issues. Because the Baptist church is so decentralized, it is often difficult to find a distinct "Baptist position." Many statements have been issued, but none of them holds binding authority for members of Baptist congregations.

The American Baptists published *Creation and the Covenant of Caring* in June 1989. This article explains the importance of Earth care and the responsibility human beings have as stewards of God's creation. The American Baptists support environmental education and an ecologically sound lifestyle. They also encourage people to do their part in shaping public policy as well as influencing industry, businesses, farmers, and consumers to maintain a healthy global environment.

The Southern Baptist Convention has not yet published an environmental statement. The official position of Southern Baptists is to strongly oppose artificial birth control. Although women are seen as equal to men, created in the image of God, they are still required to submit to the wishes of their husbands, even if the decisions made affect their own bodies. Concern for environmental degradation and growing population is slowly becoming an issue, but currently Southern Baptists remain anti-family planning and against the empowerment of women.

Most recently, the Texas Baptist Convention has separated itself from the Southern Baptist Convention. The Texas Baptist Christian Life Commission supports responsible use of Earth's resources. They acknowledge that human beings have a commitment to the natural environment. Pollution, overpopulation, and overconsumption are major issues faced by Baptists today. The Texas Baptist Christian Life Commission encourages people to use the Bible's ethical messages on creation care to preserve and protect the planet.

Catholicism and Ecology

The Roman Catholic Church historically has been pronatalist. The Vatican has officially banned all types of artificial birth control, including sterilization (Pope Paul VI 1968, Human Vital Paragraph 14 Unlawful Birth Control Methods). Nevertheless, many Catholics are becoming concerned with the environmental and social damage caused by the increasing human population. Pope Paul VI said in *Populorum Progressio* (*The Development of Peoples*) that "demographic increases" could outstrip "available resources" (Maguire 1993).

While the United States Catholic bishops recognized that "the Earth's resources are finite" (Maguire 1993), the Vatican also states that limiting birth rates is not the panacea for the environmental and social problems occurring in the world. Consumption and distribution are part of the problem.

Even though Pope John Paul II rejects a "pro-choice" position, he encourages people to become "pro-woman." Many counseling centers have seen that leaving a woman to bear the responsibilities of childbearing alone causes women to choose abortion. The Vatican encourages men to share with women the responsibilities of raising children but rejects those that claim to "help women by liberating them from the prospect of motherhood" (Pope John Paul II 1994).

Many Catholics are trying to redirect their focus from anti-abortion and anti-family planning to maintaining a balanced, sustainable population, and encouraging responsible use of Earth's resources while improving the quality of life for fellow humans in all parts of the world. Susannah Heschel explains, "The teachings of the Vatican concerning contraception and abortion may be intended only for Catholics, but the consequences of global overpopulation affect the entire human population; no religion is an island. Each of us has a stake in what the other is teaching" (Heschel 1994).

Environmental concern is new to the Catholic Church. Only recently has the Vatican issued a stance on consumption and Earth Care. Pope John Paul II spoke on ecology and caring for nature at the Celebration of the World Day of Peace. He warned that without a change in lifestyle, an increase in ecological education, and an acknowledgment of the aesthetic value of nature, modern society would find no solution to the ecological problem (Gottlieb 1996, 235). A giant step for Catholic participation in the environmental movement was the establishment of the Environmental Justice Program. This organization is active in environmental education and funding of Earth-friendly parishes (Chapman, Petersen, and Smith-Moran 2000, 133).

The Vatican holds a nationstate seat in the United Nations, and therefore has more power than other religions over the political decisions made about women, population, and the environment. Recently, Catholic women's groups and other denominational representatives have raised public questions about the Vatican's status at the United Nations.

Episcopalians and Ecology

The Episcopal Church shares concern for the state of the natural environment with many other Christian denominations. In 1973, the Episcopal Church made a resolution to encourage stewardship of the natural environment and responsible use of God's creation (General Convention 1973). Ecologically sound practices within the church, such as recycling and energy conservation, started being encouraged in 1994 (General Convention 1994). Many Episcopal Church groups work on environmental projects at the church as well as in the community.

Episcopalians recognize that the growing human population is one of the major causes of environmental degradation worldwide. Water, air, open spaces, and animals, as well as the health and well being of many human beings, are being negatively affected by rapid growth of the human population. The peace and justice of the planet are put in danger when poverty, environmental destruction and inadequate health care lead to human suffering. The Episcopal Church reaffirms the 1930 Lambeth Conference of the Angelical Communion, which approved contraception and family planning programs and facilities (General Convention 1994). In addition, Episcopalians discourage environmental racism and sexism, and promote active participation in the environmental and family planning policy process.

The Lutheran Church and Ecology

The Evangelical Lutheran Church recognizes the ecological problems facing the world today. The Lutheran environmental ethic stated in *Caring for Creation: Vision, Hope, and Justice*, explains the importance of preserving the Earth, protecting water, air and soil from pollutants, and being mindful of human consumption. "God's command to have dominion and subdue the Earth is not a license to dominate and exploit" (Evangelical Lutheran Church, September 1993). Biodiversity and species protection is also very important in protecting creation. The Sabbath is observed as a resting day not only for people, but for Earth as well.

Because of concern for the well being of children and women, the Evangelical Lutheran Church supports the use of responsible family planning by couples that do not desire, or cannot provide adequately for a child. Families that do not or cannot produce children are not to be looked down upon, as having children is not a religious requirement. Rather, it is a very personal choice of married couples (Evangelical Lutheran Church, November 1996). Abortion is permitted only after all other options have been considered, especially adoption. Abortion is also permitted if the woman's life is in danger, or if the child faces severe medical abnormalities that would cause the child to suffer or die soon after birth (Evangelical Lutheran Church, September 1991).

The United Methodist Church and Ecology

The United Methodist Church is becoming a strong force in the environmental movement. The Book of Resolutions explicitly takes a firm environmental stance that encourages sound ecological living and discourages overconsumption, unequal distribution of resources, and

> The destruction of a species is like, metaphorically, like tearing a page out of the scripture.
>
> — *Keeping the Earth*

destruction of Creation (UMC 1996). "All creation is the Lord's, and we are responsible for the ways we use and abuse it. Water, air, soil, minerals, energy resources, plants, animal life, and space are both to be valued and conserved" (UMC official website). Population and consumption are recognized as some of the major causes of human impact on the global environment.

The United Methodist Church supports the use of responsible family planning, including voluntary sterilization, as a way to lessen the destructive human impact on Earth and promote women's reproductive health. Methodist congregations are concerned with economic security, health care, and literacy for all, including women and girls. Improving the status and securing the rights of women is a priority for empowering women as well as stabilizing global population and preserving the environment (UMC 1996).

Mormonism and Ecology

Although the Church of Jesus Christ of Latter Day Saints does not have an explicit environmental ethic, many Mormons are becoming concerned with environmental degradation and overpopulation. Mormons historically were encouraged to have large families. Recently, however, the poverty, famine, and environmental destruction caused by our growing population have made many Mormon families reconsider family size. The new Church Handbook of Instructions for bishoprics and stake presidencies states that the personal decision to use birth control is left up to the couple and God (Boulder Daily Camera, December 7, 1998, C-7). Although Mormons still typically have large families, family planning allows Mormon couples to plan and space their children as they see fit, with prayer and inspiration from God. The Church of Jesus Christ of Latter Day Saints' handbook previously said nothing about birth control or sexual relations, and many Mormons support the new policy. Homer S. Ellsworth, a retired Salt Lake City obstetrician who wrote the entry in the Encyclopedia of Mormonism, stated that Mormon attitudes about sex have changed, and the new policy allows for more personal interpretation (Boulder Daily Camera).

The Mormon Church also has a strong stance on the treatment of women. Women are treated as equals in the church and are allowed to make decisions and have careers outside the home. The president of the Church of Jesus Christ of Latter Day Saints, Gordon B. Hinckley, stated, "...let me say to you sisters that you do not hold a second place in our Father's plan for the eternal happiness and well-being of His children. You are an absolutely essential part of that plan" (Hinckley 1996). Literacy, empowerment, and equality of women have a direct correlation to the size of their families and, therefore, affect the amount of environmental impact caused by humans.

The Presbyterian Church and Ecology

Because Presbyterians believe God is the ultimate owner of creation and humans are allowed to enjoy Earth because of His kindness and generosity, protecting Earth is critically important. Social justice, as well as biotic justice, is a high priority in the Presbyterian faith. Sustainability and frugality are necessary to maintain a just and ecologically friendly planet. Frugality means moderation, thrift, or temperance. This concept is similar to "contentment" in the first letter to Timothy (6:6-10). As in many other denominations, interdependence between, or connection to, all things on Earth is a major component of the Presbyterian environmental ethic.

Human rights, including women's rights, are also a priority of the Presbyterian environmental crusade. Empowerment of women and women's reproductive health are encouraged as a way to decrease birthrates and increase the status of women. For more than 30 years, Presbyterians have accepted birth control and other family planning methods as a way to support an ecologically and socially just planet. A quote from *Hope for a Global Future*, the Presbyterian study guide for moving toward a just and sustainable human development, says it best: "As followers of Jesus Christ who live in relative affluence, American Presbyterians must consider the possibility that God places a responsibility upon each of us to use all the means available to us to see that just and sustainable human development becomes a reality for the whole human family in harmony with all of

"The 'brotherhood of man' needs to be widened to embrace not only women but also the whole community of life."

— Rosemary Radford Ruether, *Sexism and God-Talk*

God's creation" (Office of the General Assembly, Presbyterian Church 1996, 89).

Unitarian Univeralists and Ecology

Unitarian Universalists combine the tenets of Christianity and Judaism to form an Earth-centered, humanistic denomination. Unitarian Universalists strive for justice and respect for every person and respect for the interdependent web of existence of which we are a part (UUA official website, Principles and Purposes). Unitarian Universalists practice Earth-centered traditions that celebrate the circle of life and instruct how to live in harmony with nature. The Flower Communion is one example of how Earth is considered sacred to Unitarian Universalists. The opening words of this ceremony tell of support from Earth: "Supported by Earth's strong, firm crust, we build our homes, till the fields, plant our gardens and our orchards...The Earth is truly our home, and we are one with all Earth's creatures..." The Flower Communion teaches adults and children the importance of diversity and gratitude for Earth's gifts.

Women also have a strong role in the Unitarian Universalists faith. They have open communication within the congregation and have their own groups specifically for advancing women's spirituality, such as Unitarian Universalist Women's Heritage Society, Womenspirit, Unitarian Universalists Acting to Stop Violence Against Women, and the Unitarian Universalist Women's Federation. Unitarian Universalists support women's empowerment and reproductive freedom. Planning of family size by using contraception is supported, and sex education of men, women, and children is encouraged.

Islam and Ecology

In the Islamic tradition, reverence for nature is found, as well as the concept that God created everything in balance. Islam teaches that humans are a part of the community of animals, birds, and every other aspect of nature. However, in many Islamic countries dissent arises over the role of women in society. In large cities of the Islamic world, such as Amman, Damascus, and Islamabad, modernization has brought acceptance of family planning. However, in the rural areas, women are still hidden away from the world and from the benefits of modern society.

Islam, like many other religions, demonstrates a concern for the state of our planet. A type of "green jihad" (holy war) is forming (Denny 1998). The Qur'an, the Islamic Holy Book, has many specific lines explaining the importance of avoiding overconsumption and of protecting the natural creation, but also has flexibility to be interpreted as society changes in time and place. Earth is actually mentioned 453 times in the Qur'an (Denny 1998). "The world is green and beautiful and God has appointed you as His stewards over it. He sees how you acquit yourselves" (Chapman, Petersen and Smith-Moran 2000, 158). As in many other religions, Islamic views differ from country to country, but the overall environmental approach is the same. Animals and plants are generally valued and protected in the Muslim faith. Women, on the other hand, have very low status in Islamic countries. Women have unequal rights in the family, in government, in marriage, and in Muslim society in general.

Over one billion people in over 80 countries practice Islam (Coward 1995, 123). Consequently, the environmental movement seeks to include Islamic people by carefully considering Muslim cultural and social requirements. Many Muslim countries are wealthy from the oil industry, an industry that is also one of the most environmentally devastating. Economics often takes precedence over environmental concerns. Nevertheless, Muslim people are concerned with their fertility and consumption as well as their effect on the health of the global environment.

Islamic nations tend to have some of the highest population growth rates in the world. The crude birth rate of forty-six Muslim countries is one percent higher than that of the developing countries as a whole (Coward and Maguire 1995, 140). The Qur'an has no exact requirements for the use of contraception, but Islamic scholars have historically discouraged family planning. Contraception is only allowed if it is not permanent and does not interfere with a woman's natural hormonal cycle (Coward 1995, 127). Infanticide is explicitly outlawed and abortion under no circumstances can be used as a method of population control (Chapman, Petersen, and Smith-Moran 2000, 160). Islamic texts do, on the other hand, permit family planning and abortion if health risks make pregnancies undesirable (Coward 1995, 127).

When family planning education is provided to couples in Islamic societies, the decline in birth rates is negligible. This is because women's status is so low. Violence, oppression, and lack of safe, effective health care are common circumstances for Islamic women and girls. The issue of who has control over women's bodies was one of the major concerns at the Cairo Conference, where many Islamic women forcefully challenged traditional Islamic views on women's rights. Dr. Riffat Hassan states that this indicates that "Muslim women are no longer nameless, faceless or voiceless and that they are ready to stand up and be counted" (CEDPA, *Interfaith reflections on women, poverty, and population*, 59). Fertility is proven to drop when women are empowered and educated. Until Muslim women are allowed to have an education, an opportunity to advance in the workforce, and more social and political freedom, the fertility of Islamic nations will remain high.

Buddhism and Ecology

A religious belief in the protection of nature is a fundamental part of both Buddhism and Hinduism. In Thailand, the Wat Phai Lom and Wat Asokaram wildlife refuges are actually Buddhist monasteries. Buddhism has always recognized the interrelatedness of humans and nature. Buddhist monks are committed to preserving the harmony of the natural environment. As a result, they are protecting the habitat of colonial nesting bird species in the midst of a rapidly growing country that is losing its coastal resources and wetlands.

Buddhism has a unique perspective on human responsibility to nature and consideration of fellow human beings. Buddhist history is full of deep appreciation for human life, animals, and plants, as well as Earth itself. Sex, population, and the environment are all addressed in the Buddhist faith, and there is a growing concern for our planet's welfare among Buddhists. The fundamental environmental ethic in Buddhism is based on two concepts: rebirth and interdependence.

Interdependence ("pratityasamutpada" in Sanskrit and "paticcasamuppada" in Pali) is a basic teaching in Buddhism and a fundamental environmental ethic that demonstrates that all beings are connected in a cause-and-effect relationship. No being is an isolated and separate entity, and an individual can make no decision without affecting the entire matrix of creatures and Earth. Therefore, decisions regarding fertility or consumption do not simply affect the person making the decisions. Rather, these decisions affect every other human, plant, and animal, as well as the natural environment. Being selfish or negligent results in receiving negative karma, so Buddhists strive to always remain conscious of their decisions, especially those decisions that are predicted to negatively affect others. "Walking the middle path," or living life in moderation, is the desired and least destructive practice. One is encouraged to enjoy life but also to avoid overconsumption or indulgence. A simple and sustainable lifestyle is encouraged in Buddhism, and a connectedness with all creatures and Earth itself is very important in the Buddhist environmental ethic.

Rebirth also affects the way Buddhists make decisions about consumption and reproduction. After death, one could come back to Earth in any form, including plant or animal. Because a person could return to Earth in any form, all creatures must be treated with respect and compassion. The Lankavantara Sutra explains: "In the long course of rebirth there is not one among living beings with form who has not been mother, father, brother, sister, son, or daughter, or some other relative. Being connected with the process of taking birth, one is kin to all wild and domestic animals, birds, and beings born from the womb" (Swearer 1998). Although human form is considered to be the highest order of rebirth, every creature, and Earth, should be treated with dignity and should have the opportunity to achieve enlightenment (nirvana).

Buddhist teachings also favor life and quality of life. Because Buddhists consider life precious, birth control is not normally an acceptable form of family planning. On the other hand, because quality of life is important, when resources cannot support a growing population, family planning is encouraged in order to deter poverty, hunger, and disease (IECH Bureau Health Division 1994). Contraception and abstinence are acceptable when resources are low, and small families are encouraged so the parents, community, and planet are not exhausted. In the current global community, resources *are* severely depleted and natural population checks (i.e. famine, disease, and poverty) seem to be an unnecessary and extreme reality. Buddhism regards reproduction as a mature choice rather than an accident or religious duty. Therefore, birth control is a safe and effective way to deter human suffering and ensure a healthy global environment (Coward 1995, 155).

Most forms of Buddhism do not portray a negative opinion of sexuality, as in many Western traditions, although all forms of Buddhism have standards for sexual ethics. In fact, in Vajrayana Buddhism, sex is a sacred act to be enjoyed, not feared. Buddhism identifies sexuality as part of human nature and human communication. According to Rita M. Gross, a practicing Buddhist and scholar trained in comparative studies in religion, "Mindful sexuality should be encouraged by all religions." She also encourages breaking the bond between sex and reproduction. By doing this, she claims, population growth will stabilize and women will gain some empowerment by supporting the concept that "female" does not automatically mean "mother." Opening talk about sexuality among people of faith and valuing sexual relationships will contribute to a caring, egalitarian relationship between women and men (Coward 1995, 155).

Buddhism places an important value on human contact with nature. Buddhist practice often takes place in natural areas to avoid distraction from the hustle of urban life ("Delightful are forests..." *The Dhammapada*, Chapter VII, The Worthy Verse 99). Monks often maintain lavish gardens at their monasteries, such as the Buddhadasa's Garden of Empowering Liberation. Planting these gardens not only shows the value of nature, but also allows for a transformation of lifestyle from technology to sustainable agriculture ("Cut down the forest! Not a tree...Having cut down both forest and underbrush, O bhikkhus, be ye without forests." *The Dhammapada*, Chapter XX, The Path Verse 283). The founder of Buddhism himself (Siddhartha) found tranquillity and concentration sitting under a tree. "Seeking the supreme state of sublime peace, I wandered...until...I saw a delightful stretch of land and a lovely woodland grove, and a clear flowing river with a delightful forest so I sat down thinking 'Indeed, this is an appropriate place to strive for the ultimate realization of...Nirvana' (*Ariya-pariyesana Sutra*, Majjhima Nikaya).

Interestingly, the national family planning program in Thailand has been credited with playing a major role in the substantial fertility decline that has occurred in that country since the mid-1960s. Thailand's total fertility rate declined from 3.2% in 1971 to 1.1% in 1998. Experts point to the spirit of innovation in contraceptive techniques and distribution as important factors contributing to the success of the Thai program (Rosenfield et al. 1982, 43). In other Buddhist-practicing countries, as well, the faith of the people has not been an obstacle to the practice of fertility reduction.

Hinduism and Ecology

The natural environment, especially trees and rivers, are considered sacred in Hinduism. The planting of trees is encouraged and the cutting of trees is condemned. Because of the large population of India, many trees have been cleared and rivers polluted anyway. Hindu environmentalists are trying to reverse the ecological damage caused by the large Indian population by donating money to the Tirumala-Tirupati Devasthanam (TTD, the office bureaucracy of the temple), which in turn uses the money to plant trees and other plants. The TTD also sells saplings to religious pilgrims at a very inexpensive price as a gift from the deity. These saplings are then planted at the pilgrim's home as if a real piece of the Tirumala sacred place is there with them (Coward and Maguire 2000, 111).

Rivers are also considered sacred places in India. It is said that if one bathes in these rivers, one is cleansed of sins (papa). Many of these sacred rivers have been damned or polluted and therefore cannot be used for ritual cleansing (Coward and Maguire 2000, 111).

Women are seen as a valuable component of nature. Rivers in India are said to be female because they nurture and feed Earth. In a small Indian village near Kumbakonam, the River Kaveri floods after the monsoon rains, watering the newly planted crops that will eventually feed everyone in the area. The Kaveri River is regarded as pregnant and the villagers celebrate the river's fertility by having picnics by the riverbank. Now this river is dammed and no longer flows through the agricultural villages.

Hindu women have also been very active in the ecological movement. Because women are among the people most severely affected by environmental damage, they have had a strong influence on environmental policy. One example of this is the Chipko ("tree-huggers") movement, in which women wrapped their arms around trees needed for watershed and food, refusing to let loggers destroy important natural areas. Many Indian women were killed trying to save what they knew were valuable natural ecosystems (Breton 1998, 3).

Almost all Hindu texts celebrate having children, especially boys. Nevertheless, the Indian government has installed an aggressive family planning program that many Hindu families accept. But high infant mortality rates and poor treatment of women tends to lead to high fertility. India has one of the highest infant mortality rates in the world. Until health care and nutritious food is made available to everyone and empowerment of women becomes a priority, the Hindu population will continue to rise.

Indigenous Spirituality and Ecology

Indigenous tradition commonly includes some type of preservation, conservation or ecological responsibility to the natural world. Many indigenous groups display a kinship with or supernatural respect for land, animals and ecosystems. Indigenous hunters and farmers often utter blessings or prayers before cutting down a tree or killing an animal. For example, a Kwagiuti hunter would give praise to a slain animal for its sacrifice, saying: "Greetings friend that we have met, only to destroy you my friend. Apparently the creator created you so that I could hunt you to feed myself and my wife, my friend" (Coward 1995, 63).

Indigenous groups rely heavily on the natural environment and know the areas in which they live very well.

Gandhi said: "As human beings our greatness lies not so much in being able to remake the world—that is the myth of the Atomic Age—as in being able to remake ourselves."

— *Population, Consumption and Ecology,* Hessel and Ruether, editors

Most groups acknowledge the integrity of natural resources and the intimate relationships that exists between all living and nonliving things. A brotherhood with Earth is not uncommon. Luther Standing Bear, author of *Land of the Spotted Eagle* and member of the Lakota nation, stated a teaching that is common to many indigenous peoples: "All this was in accordance with the Lakota belief that man did not occupy a special place in the eyes of Wakan Tanka, the Grandfather of us all. I was only part of everything that was called the world" (Grim 1998).

Among the Yoruba of Nigeria and Brazil, a high prize is placed on children because of the high infant mortality in their culture. Fertility is a sign of blessing, as in the ancient days of Judeo-Christian society. A child is not considered human until named. In many other cultures, a child is often not named until they reach the age of five.

The richness of the Yoruba ethical teachings is part of an oral tradition, now captured in the *Odu Ifa*. The ethical framework of the *Odu Ifa* is: 1) the dignity of the human; 2) the well being of family and community; 3) the integrity of the environment; and 4) the community of shared human interests (Karenga, xi). The dignity and power of women is described in these writings as well.

"And when he gave her power, he gave her the spirit power of the bird. It was then that he gave women the power and authority so that anything men wished to do, they could not dare to do it successfully without women" (Karenga, 73).

Few other religious teachings give women such a prominent place of honor. In Brazil, the Mae de Santo, Mother Saint or High Priestess, is chiefly charged with religious ceremony. Later references speak of the belief that any childbearing woman can give birth to a priest or even God (Karenga, 219). It was this process which could bring heaven to Earth.

As in these examples of indigenous spirituality, modern theologians and philosophers argue that the survival of humanity is dependent upon maintaining the integrity of a natural system that is vital to the survival of all species. Within the formal religious community today, there is a growing emphasis on responsibility for renewing and redefining the human role in relation to the Earth and its systems.

New Religious Perspectives

Newer religious perspectives are found in "deep ecology," the Gaia theory, creation spirituality and experiential gatherings. With humans' recent renewed understanding of the value of nature has come the realization that human population must be maintained at a level that ensures human dignity and quality of life as well. This has led the deep ecology movement to include population as one of its basic principles.

I will sing of well-founded Gaia, Mother of All, eldest of beings, she feeds all creatures that are in the world, all that go upon the goodly land and all that are in the paths of the sea, and all that fly: all these are fed of her store.

— Homeric Hymn, 7th Century B.C.

> The flourishing of human life and cultures is compatible with a substantial decrease of the human population. The flourishing of nonhuman life requires such a decrease (Devall 1985, 70).

Gaia refers to the Greek Earth Goddess, and the Gaia theory proposes that the Earth is a living system. The Gaia movement dates back to the writings of James Lovelock and later Lynn Margulis. The Gaia concept is fundamentally a biological viewpoint that does not necessarily serve the purposes of a religious doctrine. Human population growth is seen as only a small part of human history. From the Gaian view, humans are as likely to become extinct as other species.

Creation spirituality springs from the work of mystics in the Middle Ages: Hildegard von Bingen, Meister Eckhart, Rumi and many others. Their mysticism is grounded in creation. While celebrating the joy of Earth and all its creatures, those individuals who are steeped in creation spirituality are pursuing justice for humans and for the planet. Compassion becomes the motivating force. "Compassion is the alternative way of seeing the universe, and compassion is fifty percent about celebration and fifty percent about healing and social justice making" (Fox 1994, 278). This approach requires a great commitment to challenge the old structures of institutional society, culture and religion. The future is a dance, no less mysterious than the past or present. But re-imagining and re-imaging the world and humans' space in it poses the most creative venture of all.

Finally, a proliferation of organizations, institutes and associations are providing a mix of religious, psychological and environmental workshops and conferences for people looking at alternative spiritual experiences. These events are often termed ecopsychology, although the principles of ecology, psychology and theology seemed to be merged in both didactic and experiential formats. The growing popularity of these types of meetings indicates a demand for a new way to integrate religious expression into daily life. While some pursue their religious expression through meetings, others are redeeming the ancient practices of women-based faiths. Groups dedicated to the principles of the feminine Earth find healing by going back to the most ancient of matrifocal ritual.

The Principles of Justice

Where the religious and ethical groups should be able to come together is around the concept of justice. Ultimately, most concerns today about population growth and resource consumption come through a human being-centered approach (anthropocentrism) to looking at the world. However, many of the traditional spiritual attitudes of people were biocentric. Nature was honored and revered because the health of land was tied to the health and survival of people. How do we bind these ideas to a future that is healthy for nature and for people?

Even the most conservative Western religious faiths recognize population growth as an issue in relation to the environment. Divisions arise over the means of dealing with population growth and related issues of fertility regulation. And although we search for harmony with nature on the one hand, we propose to intervene in the natural processes on the other. The principles of justice become critical: social, ecological, and intergenerational.

Social Justice

The domestication of compassion took place especially with the industrial revolution when morality came to mean bedroom morality because the real issues of injustice, such as work, unemployment, child labor, were removed entirely from home or church into the market place (Fox 1979, 14).

You can hold yourself back from the suffering of the world: this is something you are free to do... but perhaps precisely this holding back is the only suffering you might be able to avoid. – Franz Kafka (Macy 1991, 21)

The different approaches to life and to nature of all countries are important in considering the economic disparity faced by the poorest of poor. Often the issues of the environment become diffused in the face of poverty and inequity. The most troubling issue of this time of the greatest prosperity on Earth is the presence of a level of poverty for over one billion of Earth's inhabitants that rivals any period in history, if only because of the numbers.

Consider some of the facts:

◆ Child labor, dilapidated housing, crime and class tension are documented in megacities worldwide (PRB 2000).

◆ In 31 countries people face chronic shortage of fresh water supplies that threaten their health and living standards (PRB).

◆ One child under 5 years of age dies from hunger and related causes every 2.7 seconds (PRB).

◆ More than 800 million people worldwide do not get enough to eat (PRB).

◆ One-third of the world's children under the age of 5 is underweight (PRB).

◆ Sixty percent of infant mortality is linked to water-related infectious and parasitic diseases (PLANet 2000).

◆ Eight hundred million people are unemployed or

underemployed in developing countries—more than the entire workforce of the industrialized world (PLANet).

- More than a million motherless children are left behind each year because of maternal mortality (PLANet).
- Infant mortality is 10 times higher in developing countries than developed countries.
- 585,000 women die—at least one every minute of every day—related to pregnancy and childbirth—99% of these in developing nations (PLANet).
- More than 40 percent of all sub-Saharan Africans live below the poverty line (PRB).

Where is the hope in these dire figures? For many, social equity concerns should receive primary attention, before other issues like population or environment. In the social justice movement, population policy has relevance only if such a policy *ensures gender and social justice*. There is a belief that fewer people will not lead to less poverty, nor that all social problems begin as population problems.

Others argue that there is an undeniable relationship between "numbers" and inequities. With all other conditions remaining the same, and numbers increasing, inevitably inequities will increase. The debate has often been framed in terms of numbers versus individual human rights. However, the 1994 International Conference on Population and Development held by the United Nations in Cairo, Egypt, made major contributions to redefining the approach to population, economics and environment. Utilizing language from Agenda 21, the working action plan from the environmental Earth Summit, the ICPD Programme of Action incorporated explicit goals for improving economic well-being, preserving environmental integrity, improving the status of women and providing health care, especially reproductive health care for all people.

The ICPD Programme of Action also gives some discussion to the role of wasteful production and consumption in industrialized countries. Overall U.S. consumption patterns remain unacceptable to the world community—even with zero population growth. Elements of social justice can be found in the attention U.S.

citizens give to reducing the impact of their lifestyles on the global environment. The average North American consumes three times the freshwater, 10 times the energy and 19 times the aluminum of someone in a developing country (Durning 1992). And citizens in the U.S. use up to six times the world's per capita average in energy resources. (*Audubon* 1994).

Unfortunately, many U.S. citizens believe it is their "right" to consume or at least enjoy the riches of the new economic prosperity. Ironically, in the United States estimates exist that 13.5 million or five percent of the U.S. population have been homeless at some point in their lives. Economic prosperity is not guaranteed for all, even in our own country.

Ecological Justice

A land ethic changes the role of Homo Sapiens *from conqueror of the land-community to plain member and citizen of it. It implies respect for his fellow-members, and also respect for the community as such.* –Aldo Leopold.

We see it as our duty to speak as caretakers for the natural world. Government is a process of living together, the principle being that all life is equal, including the four-legged and the winged things. The principle has been lost; the two-legged walks about thinking he is supreme with his manmade laws. But there are universal laws of all living things. We come here and we say they too have rights. –Chief Oren Lyons.

The second type of justice is ecological in nature, hence the term: ecojustice. What is ecojustice? The term means justice for all life on the planet. Although under traditional moral codes the concept of justice was limited to humans, today ecojustice is expanded to include responsibility for all life. This concept of respect for life is part of the traditional culture of many countries.

To underline the need for ecojustice, the following facts come from another Audubon document, *Population and Habitat in the New Millennium*, written by

"It is, after all, the ecological barbarians of the world who refer to themselves as developed."

— Daniel C. Maguire, *Ethics for a Small Planet*

Kenneth Strom (1998).

- In the past 40 years we consumed 1/3 of the forests that existed in 1950 (Raven 1994).
- We are clearing tropical forests around the globe at the rate of over 200 square miles per day (Harrison 1992).
- If current trends continue, in 40 years only 25% of the world's coral reefs will remain intact and functioning (Hinricksen 1997).
- Every 20 minutes another species of life becomes extinct (Wilson 1992).
- At least 27,000 species are lost each year (Wilson 1992).
- At least 16% of U.S. bird species are in decline (http://www.audubon.org/bird/watch).
- At least ½ of all species migrating to Latin America have exhibited significant declines in recent years (Youth 1994).

Respect for the land and other members of the land-community extend through the work of many modern "nature" writers. The prose, often poetic and filled with emotion, gives rise to some innate connection to the creativity of Earth and all its creatures. Some of Loren Eisley's most moving essays are found in *The Immense Journey*, where he traces the evolution of man and nature through time. Capturing the wonder of the Earth and its processes, one can begin to appreciate what the community of nature is that humans participate in and what we might lose. Life is connected in a circle of time and space, with every species playing a unique role.

Henryk Skolimowski, professor of philosophy at the University of Michigan, presents it thus, "If the cosmic web embraces us all, if it is woven of the strands of which we are part, then justice to the cosmic web means justice to all its elements—to all brothers and sisters of creation, as native Americans would say." It is this circularity of connectedness that is framing much of the new science. Feedback loops in biology and physics underline the concept of a web that includes all species and systems (Capra 1996, 56).

Interviews with environmentally conscious citizens expose an intense need to physically move out of every-day life and into a closer juxtaposition with the natural world. Each person experiences a heightened awareness of connection with other species, and some describe a dissolution of individual identity (Waak 1998, 25). Descriptions of animal/human relationships abound, either through the domestication of birds, dogs, cats and other animals or through active work with wild species like bears, wolves and ecotourism in wildlife areas.

The compassion expressed through social justice finds a place among these people in the concern for ecojustice. At times these forms of justice come into confrontation. Those who are moved by the sight of a starving child may be removed from the images of bulldozed rain forests. This situation, oft repeated in developing countries, presents us with an important question. Can the concept of ecojustice be accommodated to the needs of countries for economic development?

Prior to the arrival of colonial and Western influence, many Africans held a reverence for nature and natural places. Humans and nature lived in harmony. Some of this continues to this day. In Zimbabwe, where human population growth was at a level of 3%, the Marange on Mapembe Mountain continue to guard their sacred places and restrict the number of people living in the area. The mountain is associated with long-held beliefs of spiritual wisdom and power. The Zimbabwean officials at the Department of Natural Resources term this protection "cultural conservation," but it is the common way that people around the world, despite poverty and inequity, have protected their traditions.

In Zimbabwe, as in many parts of Africa, nature has become an economic commodity. Governmental regulations over poaching of wildlife has often resulted in armed conflict. Innovative programs related to wildlife use and conservation for local villages have increased the ability of the people to reap the benefits, while giving them control over the protection of the natural resources. The intrinsic value of nature has not been forgotten.

A pygmy legend recounts the story of the little boy who finds a bird that sings a beautiful song in the forest. He brings it home. He asks his father to bring food for the bird. The father does not want to feed a little bird, so he kills it. The man immediately drops dead. So, the legend says, the

*man killed the bird, and with the bird he
killed the song, and with the song he killed
himself. When human beings destroy their
environment, they destroy their own
nature too.*

The Power of Myth
(Joseph Campbell with Bill Moyers, 21-22)

By contrast, population growth in the interior western United States has made the confrontation between people and bears an increasing problem. Driven by overlapping and encroaching habitat, the bears come to houses to feed on garbage, bird feeders and gardens of the new human inhabitants. The result is that the bears will often be destroyed by wildlife managers in order to prevent future human and bear confrontations.

Poverty is not the only reason that humans and wildlife come into conflict. Affluence, which is defined as living in a wild area on spacious property, can produce a situation between humans and wildlife where the wildlife loses. Ecojustice then must be demonstrated in a way that provides space for wild things, whether they be plants or animals.

Intergenerational Justice

The saying of the indigenous people of Latin America that humans today are borrowing their children's future applies to the future of other species as well. In essence, the human community is actually "closing down the savings accounts" for many forms of life on the planet.

Intergenerational justice asks individuals to look far into the future. It entails a process of "ecovision:" envisioning a future that is healthy and sustainable for all generations. It requires anticipating the problems of the grandchildren and great-grandchildren. It necessitates asking the question, "If I were alive 100 years from now, what would I want the world to be like?" Most of all, it requires planning and action.

The World Commission on Environment and Development asked that the needs of the present be met without compromising the ability of future generations to meet their own needs. These needs include the right to participate fully and with equity in a basic quality of life for all people, which cannot be achieved if the resources of the planet are completely consumed. It cannot be achieved without a major restructuring of the world economy. It probably cannot be achieved without a better understanding of the concept of stewardship and what that means for our daily lives. It surely cannot be achieved without a partnership between rich and poor, young and old, Christian and Buddhist and all other people of faith.

So here are some things we must do for the sake of future generations, if not for our own:

◆ Reduce the use of fossil fuels and find non-polluting sources of energy.

◆ Reduce deforestation of critical biodiverse regions of the world and reforest areas with native trees and plants.

◆ Stop pollution of water supplies, reduce demand for fresh water, and find new methods of efficient agricultural irrigation.

◆ Increase the ability of farmers to grow subsistence crops, reduce use of chemicals and pesticides, and create better food distribution programs.

◆ Reduce the incidence of infectious and parasitic diseases worldwide.

◆ Increase health care for individuals, especially women and children, including the means to practice voluntary child spacing and birth control.

◆ Reduce wasteful production and consumption of all natural resources, especially on the part of industrialized countries.

◆ Make space for wild creatures and habitat.

◆ Provide hope for our children.

Finding Consensus for Partnership

As we have seen in almost all the countries of the world, the traditional ethic of care for nature abounds in our religious beliefs. These same countries have practices that support programs to stabilize population. However, the means for designing the world we envision are varied. The following section attempts to identify some of the issues which keep the development and religious communities from working together and must be the starting point for reconciliation.

Fundamental religious, moral or ethical considerations arise most often in the discussion of certain specific issues: resource distribution, resource consumption, "population control" and coercion, culture and tradition, freedom of choice about family size, the value of females, the rights of women, and the morality of abortion. The intent of this discussion is to encourage a healthy consideration of these points with a hope for understanding and consensus.

Resource Distribution

The most foresighted evaluation of U.S. demographic prospects, *Population and the American Future*, estimated the effects that slower population growth would have on poverty in the United States in the year 2000. The commission found that the general improvement in average income associated with slower population growth would assist in reducing poverty, but would not eliminate it (Rockeller Commission Report 1972). As we begin the 21st century, it is clear that population growth has slowed and that poverty has declined. However, the process is much more complex in poorer countries.

Developing countries are hard-pressed to provide basic human needs and services to their citizens. Modest gains in production and economic growth are often diluted or negated by high rates of population growth, discouraging any reasonable hopes for a better life. Eighty percent of the world's population still lives with per capita incomes well below an adequate level of survival.

Resource distribution is a matter for heated debate in international meetings, with a split between wealthy Northern countries and poorer Southern countries. Who pays for development? How can poorer countries attain the lifestyle of richer ones?

The dilemma of poverty in relation to environment and population can be best summed up in the words of a former president of the World Conservation Union.

> "We cannot save the freshness of the air or the purity of the water or the goodness of the Earth, we cannot save the forests or the elephants or the whales, unless we save the people. We cannot ask endangered people

to rescue the planet from the many threats it faces unless we link Earth's salvation to their own. Poverty threatens the survival of the poorest. To appeal to them to join in saving the planet is pointless unless we link it to their own survival. Simply to tell those at the margin of existence not to cut down the forest or not to have as many children when they see both as necessary to their survival is to be not only insensitive to their predicament but also downright provocative. The poor need to share in the human commitment to change so that life on the planet can be sustainable for all. But to make an appeal for that commitment credible, the rest of the world must address not merely its own salvation but the relief of poverty as well" (Ramphal 1992, 143).

Can national governments reach consensus on a commitment to more equitable resource distribution? How do we link saving the planet to our own survival, especially as it relates to poorer people in the world? What steps can a community take to ensure more equitable distribution of resources?

Resource Consumption

The global environment connected resource consumption to population growth. Per capita use of oil grew 3,500 percent in the first half of the 20th century (Weber 1994, 17). By 1994, the United States accounted for 25% of the world's oil consumption. The burning of fossil fuels is a major producer of greenhouse gas emissions; therefore, it is not surprising that by 1987 the United States led other countries in the production of these discharges to the atmosphere, contributing 17.6% of the total.

Energy is a commonly used measure of resource consumption, but there are other resources which also comprise the global commons, including oceans, forests, minerals, and soil. The issue of wastes and their disposal affects individual countries, regions, and shared global resources.

As we discuss the need to stabilize population growth, those discussions must include the reduction of unsustainable consumption. The question is one of equity between countries and within countries.

Are industrialized countries willing to reduce and/ or eliminate unsustainable patterns of production and consumption? Can the religious community help to clarify options for reducing wasteful practices? How can a community become environmentally sustainable?

Population Control

In mature ecosystems, population control is the rule. In the interaction among species, plant and animal populations are regulated through a number of different relationships within the food chain.

Humans have developed more complicated brains and have molded their physical and technological environments in ways that stretch the biological rules that govern non-human species. Many people today, therefore, believe that humans can live outside the boundaries of these systems. This idea raises ethical, as well as practical, debates.

The use of the term "population control" to describe efforts towards stabilizing human population growth raises serious questions. Who is the controller and who is the controlled? Controlling for the benefit of whom?

The term "population control" implies to some people a belief that human population growth alone is responsible for environmental degradation, and therefore, it is acceptable to ignore the rights of individuals in order to slow population growth and protect the environment. In fact, population growth cannot be isolated from factors such as poverty, lack of education and health care, unjust land tenure policies, and overconsumption of natural resources by the wealthy. All of these factors must be addressed in our efforts to foster environmentally sustainable development.

More importantly, the path to stabilization of the world's population encompasses giving people, especially women, control—not taking it from them. A woman in the developing world is the center of her environment. She is the primary natural resource manager and food provider. She knows the needs of her family and her community. In order to effectively manage her life and her environment, every woman must have the right and the means to make informed decisions regarding the number and spacing of her children.

Can we trust women to control their lives and can we trust governments to listen to the wisdom of their people? Can we create new language that adequately allows women and families to be empowered by their own insights into the needs of their homes and communities?

Coercion

Coercion of any type is a violation of basic human rights and unacceptable to almost everyone. Reports of forced sterilization in many countries have surfaced over the past thirty years, from the United States to India.

Although almost no countries today have policies that demand or condone forced sterilization, abortion or birth control, many countries have a system of incentives and disincentives in regard to these practices. Incentive systems can be abused and must be carefully monitored.

Another form of coercion might be the denial of education, health care and family planning services. In the view of some, the demand that all women have as many children as possible can be seen as a form of coercion. From an ethical perspective, everything possible must be done, through policy and practice, to respect individual rights and dignity.

Can we help governments make a commitment to truly voluntary family planning?

Respect for Culture and Tradition

Prior to colonial rule in Africa, births were often spaced by means of traditional rules and practices. Modernization in many countries has disrupted the natural rhythm of the culture.

The most effective approach to issues related to population and the environment, including the delivery of reproductive health and family planning services, is to involve local people in the identification of the problems and the implementation of solutions. Local people can best adapt the approaches for sustainable development into their own culture and make them appropriate to community mores.

Can we adapt our development programs by using the knowledge of the local people? How can communities promote understanding of cultural mores?

Freedom of Choice About Family Size

Each couple and individual should be able to freely and responsibly decide on the number and spacing of their children. Freedom of choice includes information and education about life options and access to reproductive health and safe methods of fertility regulation. Freedom of choice also includes a system for informed consent.

Can we enable people to exercise their right to decide the number and spacing of children?

The Value and Rights of Women

The fundamental issue of the debate about contraception and abortion is whether women can be trusted to make moral decisions. In some ways this is puzzling, because in most societies women are entrusted with the birthing and care of the children, the tilling of the land, the keeping of the home. The conflict over how women are viewed and respected is basic to any ethical discussion about population and environment, and its resolution will be the cornerstone of a world committed to sustainable living.

In villages and towns around the world, women understand the relationship between people and the land. Opportunities available to women for education, employment and improved status will serve to strengthen the family and ensure a healthy generation of children.

This fundamental approach is also essential in improving the overall value of female children. A worldwide phenomenon of abuse, neglect, starvation, selective abortion, and even infanticide of female girls underlines the need to change attitudes.

Can we provide women and girls with the means to improve their lives?

Abortion

Although the use of artificial means of contraception creates problems with some in the religious community, the issue of abortion is by far the most controversial topic when we address issues related to population. Debate revolves around the exact moment in which the embryo becomes an individual life with a soul. For many religious groups, abortion is murder at any time after conception. For others, the time at which life becomes viable outside of the mother's womb is the moment to mark. Given current medical technology, the viability question is ever changing. Still others weigh the morality of abortion against the morality of bringing an unwanted child into the world, especially with the rise of cases of neglect and abuse prevalent today.

The reality is that abortion is legal in the United States and many other countries in the world. That legality has made the choice for abortion an issue of civil rights. Most medical practitioners believe that the incidence of abortion is a result of the failure to educate people about birth control and/or to provide the means for avoiding unintended pregnancies.

In many countries where abortion may not be legal, it is nevertheless always present. The practice of abortion often exists outside of the health system. The procedure is performed by local village midwives or an individual woman who uses unsafe, unsterile implements.

In poor countries, the medical profession, formal and informal, is more likely to have to deal with the consequences of incomplete or septic abortions which pose a major threat to the mother's life.

Can we provide women with the means to prevent pregnancy rather than terminate it? Can we trust women to make moral decisions?

Conclusion

Religious leaders, communities of conscience, environmental activists, and women's health advocates all have the desire to promote a world that is healthy for individuals. That desire must be transmitted into action for the benefit of all life on the Earth. Finding consensus on fundamental issues of conflict is the beginning of the process. This guide should be used to provoke dialogue, raise questions, and design solutions.

A resource guide of materials is provided at the back. We hope you will add to the resources any important documents we may have missed. Other comments and suggestions would also be most appreciated. Audubon has a number of policy papers, books and videotapes on the subject of population and environment. Although this guide is the work of Audubon, other groups are interested in a dialogue on these issues. We hope communities will work with all of us on finding consensus on population and environment issues and will help in exploring the ways that people of faith, concerned with justice, can shape a more just and healthy society.

Appendix

For further information about Audubon's Population & Habitat Program, or for information about Planet Awakening workshops, please write or call:

> Population & Habitat Program
> Audubon
> 4730 Table Mesa Drive, Suite I
> Boulder CO 80305
> 800.741.9658
> population@audubon.org
> http://www.audubonpopulation.org

To contact Audubon's national offices, please write or call:

> Audubon
> 700 Broadway
> New York NY 10003
> 212.979.3000
> http://www.audubon.org

To contact the PLANet campaign please visit:

> www.familyplanet.org

Sample Sermons and Other Readings

Matters of Consequence

Adapted from "The Day of Six Billion-October 12, 1999" sermon, Religious Coalition for Reproductive Choice and the Center for Reproductive Law and Policy.

According to some calculations, October 12, 1999 was the day when the six billionth person was born. Never before have there been so many people on Earth at one time. And it has happened relatively quickly. It took all of human history until 1804 for the population to reach its first billion. In 1960, we were three billion. We have doubled our number in just thirty-three years. Six billion, we are told, is a matter of consequence.

What do all these numbers tell us?

In the wonderful book *The Little Prince,* by Antoine de St. Exupery, the little prince travels from planet to planet to add to his knowledge. On one planet he finds a man who spends all of his time counting and has reached the number of five hundred and one million. "Five hundred and one million what?" asks the little prince. The man, annoyed at the interruption, answers, "Millions of those little objects which one sometimes sees in the sky." "Flies?" asks the little prince. "Oh, no," says the man. "Little golden objects that set lazy me to idle dreaming." "Ah, you mean the stars," says the little prince. "And what do you do with five hundred million stars?" The man explains that he writes the number on a little paper and then puts the paper in a drawer and locks it. "I am concerned with matters of consequence: I am accurate." The little prince is puzzled. For what is of consequence to the little prince is a flower that he waters every day and three volcanoes that he cleans out every week, since he is of use to the flower and of use to the volcanoes. And these, he announces to the man, are matters of consequence.

So as we reached the Day of Six Billion, it was, and is, useful to consider what are matters on consequence. The number six billion alone provokes fear and wonder. What will happen? How can we possibly gain control of this situation?

The real issue is not the numbers. The real issue is the quality of life of every one of the six billion. This is a matter of consequence in the eyes of God and of man. Behind that huge number of six billion are children with hopes and men with expectations and women with ideals—people all over the world who look at the stars and dream of better lives, of safe lives and fulfilling lives. Behind the numbers are names and prayers and loved ones.

The opening chapters of the book of Genesis show us a God who loves and values all of creation. Men and women are created in the image of God and regarded equally by God. They equally share the responsibility of stewardship for Earth (Genesis 1:26-28). After the flood, God makes a covenant with the descendants of Noah and with "every living creature" (Genesis 9: 9-10). If we are to be good stewards of Earth, we must strive to make our planet just and sustainable for all. We must care about and care for each of the six billion—and more to come.

For many more are to come. The United Nations projects that there will be nine billion people on Earth in just fifty years. How will we deal with this matter of consequence? God's covenant with Abraham and Sarah demonstrates that human life and reproduction are intended by God to be a blessing for the world. By promising to make their descendants "as numerous as the stars of heaven and as the sand that is on the sea-shore," God intended to bless all the nations of the world through them (Genesis 22: 17-18).

The proper stewardship of human reproduction should result in a blessing for the peoples of the world and for Earth in general. For this reason, we must strive to ensure that the birth of each child is a blessing for that child, for his or her family, and for the world in general. We must strive to ensure that families have reproductive choices that they may freely make—including family planning and contraception for all, regardless of their ability to pay; safe, legal and affordable reproductive health services; and realistic sexuality education. We must eliminate violence against women—for violence makes a mockery of our efforts to ensure women have choices. We must insist on—and work for—women's full equality. Putting women's rights first is a matter of consequence, not only for women and not only for human rights, but for the future development of the world.

At the heart of God's covenant at Mount Sinai is a fundamental concern for the poor and the well being of the land. We in the United States have too often not been good and just stewards of our planet. When we have thought about population growth, we have often blamed developing countries such as India and China. We have often avoided thinking about the excessive consumption of the wealthy countries. The affluent few have perpetuated most of the environmental degradation in the world. Our nation has the highest population growth rate in the industrialized world and one of the highest consumption rates. This is surely a matter of consequence. We must learn to live more simply so that others may simply live.

Half of the six billion people on the planet are youths, under the age of 25. More than 95 percent of them live in developing countries in Africa, Asia, and Latin America. Many of them will have difficulties finding jobs and raising and educating their children. Arable land is getting scarce and there isn't enough health care. What will their lives be like?

Half of the six billion people on the planet are women and girls, who are poorer, less educated, and less likely to have decent jobs than men. In many countries, girls are discriminated against in the most harmful ways—by getting less food, less education, and less health care than boys get. What will their lives be like?

Numbers, as the little prince knew, are not the

problem and are not a solution. The solution for us as we mark six billion is to communicate support for reproductive rights and reproductive health care at home and around the world, to our legislators and government officials. Our government should move full speed ahead to ratify international treaties that provide for women's autonomy. We should provide funding for international family planning and insist that women in the United States have access to all forms of contraception and reproductive health services. We must make good on our promises to our own citizens of quality education and equality for all.

As we think of six billion, let us begin to tear down the walls, the discriminatory laws, and the ignorance that prevents women at home and worldwide from embracing full and complete lives. Let us see that every one of the six billion women, men, and children on Earth today is accorded full human rights. In this way, we will be of use, as if we are watering a flower and cleaning out volcanoes. And these, as we know, are matters of consequence.

Let us conclude with the vision of the prophet Isaiah (65:20-23), which has never been more appropriate than it is today.

"No more shall there be in (the world) an infant that lives but a few days, or an old person who does not live out a lifetime. They shall build houses and inhabit them; they shall plant vineyards and eat their fruit. They shall not build and another inhabit: they shall not plant and another eat; for like the days of a tree shall the days of my people be, and my chosen shall long enjoy the work of their hands. They shall not labor in vain or bear children in calamity: for they shall be offspring blessed by the Lord—and their descendants as well."

Mother Earth and Mother Woman

Adapted from a speech by Guadalupe Arizpe De La Vega, President, Mexican Federation of Private Associations of Health and Community Development (FEMAP) for the National Audubon Society Road from Cairo Conference, Miami, Florida, 1994.

We believe that the destiny and survival of the human species have depended on the use of Mother Earth and Mother Woman. The first carries within her seeds that provide food and resources; the second carries within her the seeds of human life. The first nourishes us with plants, minerals, air and ecological resources; the second generates human beings nourished by the fruits of the soil.

The new ecology should be based on the balance between these mothers for survival of the planet and of life, as we know it. At this historical moment, we are facing a crisis and we hear the anguished cry of these mothers. The womb of mother earth is being eroded by our irresponsible behavior toward the environment. The wombs of the majority of our mothers in this world are exploited and abused by excessive fertility, violence, neglect and abuse.

In spite of our limitations, together men and women in the world must establish a culture that will free us from these depredations, from the abuse of the resources of life. We must reach the delicate balance between the resources of mother earth and the needs of human life in order to guarantee the harmony of that interface. It is on the philosophy of respect toward mother earth and mother woman that the efforts of responsible ecology, population growth and development must be based.

The act of reproduction should be an act of responsibility, a conscientious decision made by both partners in a sexual relationship. However, if women are not aware of the implications of conception, then reproduction becomes a brutal imposition of sexual power instead of a loving expression of sexual harmony.

In our age, the procreation and preservation of life have been greatly affected by science and technology. Before modern technology emerged, control over human population was exercised through natural calamities such as earthquakes, floods and epidemics that destroyed great segments of populations. The advent of preventive and curative medicine, including immunizations, the development of antibiotics and drugs, and the sanitation of water and food, decreased mortality rates providing humans with greater control over disease. As a result, infant mortality diminished and the span of life was prolonged.

These scientific achievements have shown us how crucial it is for the human species to develop a realistic awareness of the responsible use of our resources. It is not possible to utilize science and technology to protect life and improve natural resources, unless they are also used to provide women with more control over their own bodies and destinies. It is for this reason that the balance between population, consumption and technology must be framed within an interactive conceptual paradigm with respect for human dignity and for the empowerment of women, who are the sources of human life.

Rather than conceiving the interface of these elements in a mechanical fashion, I wish to share with you our convictions that such a delicate balance depends upon the respect for the right of persons to make responsible decisions. I am convinced that in spite of our diversity in culture, theoretical orientation, value systems and attitudes, we women are alike because we have been endowed with the capacity to create life. It is for this reason that the earth and women are complementary polarities for the ecological balance between resources and people.

Certain cultures provide interesting alternatives to the Western paradigm of exhaustion and overutilization and serve as models for how to treat the earth. For instance, in Meso-America, the Mayans used to perform a religious rite before the planting season. In this ceremony, they asked mother earth for forgiveness for the wounds they inflicted on her when plowing the land.

Other cultures, such as the ancient Egyptians, depicted the relationship between women and the Earth in beautiful ways. Nout, the daughter of Shou and Tefnout, is the wife of Geb, the Earth God. She personifies the heavenly sphere, and in the bas-reliefs of her figure are portrayed a woman whose feet rest on the eastern horizon while her body curves over the Earth and her over-stretched arms touch the boundaries of dreamland.

Above, the stars navigate the entire length of her body, and under her body, the Earth feeds its people. Every night she is charged with sheltering the disc of the sun Ra to sleep within her womb. The next day at the advent of dawn, she delivers it again to the world. Night is the sleep of the sun in her womb and dawn is the daily rebirth of light. This daily cycle of night and day takes place within her body as the genesis of life.

Carl Jung states that these cosmological visions of women, earth and fertility are part of our collective unconscious. The foundation of religious beliefs in which the human amazement at the fruits of the earth, as well as the creative powers of womanhood, led them to the naming of feminine deities. The paradox is that their treatment of feminine deities and the treatment given to women of flesh and bone was quite different. While the goddesses were wrapped in gold and worshipped in reverence, real women toiled and were abused in labor and pregnancy.

The issues related to treatment of the women and the earth have been pondered for centuries. These issues have not only been part of our times. To the human predicament of poverty, powerlessness and unequal distribution of resources, add the ecological crisis and we face a panorama, which requires great determination. The pivotal elements are human beings, their attitudes, self-concepts, respect toward others and awareness of the imbalances of the world. If we have the capacity to change those psychological elements and the resolution of humans to take control of their lives, we will have the beginnings of a great ecological and demographic revolution.

In spite of the complexity of our problems, the world will prevail and not perish; people will bloom and not decay. We need an optimistic vision of what is to come. We need to promote creative leadership, which will utilize values rather than exercise power, which will promote the creative forces within rather than control from without. We need to breathe in freedom rather than suffocate in our own limitations.

Saving the Planet

Two ethical choices: How much of "the Planet" should we use? Can it be okay to be a greedy consumer?

Copyright June 16, 2000 - Dennis Phillips, Unitarian Universalist presentation

In discussions over the past thirty-five years concerning "Saving the Planet," I've found that one important question is never asked, and that another usually receives simplistic pat answers, which deserve to be challenged. My intent today is to present the nature of "the problem" as I see it, some assumptions concerning that problem and some possible solutions, and two perhaps radical conclusions for each of you to respond to.

The first assumption I'm making, and asking that you might accept for today, is that the Biosphere is a prime basis for value in making decisions about our species, our social and economic systems, and some of our personal choices. This assumption has some things in common with the supposed Native American custom of having someone always speak for "the Seventh Generation." The major difference is that the latter is in theory intrinsically Anthropocentric, while the former could potentially even lead to the conclusion (such as that made by the Voluntary Human Extinction Movement, VHMENT, in Portland) that humans should remove themselves from the planet. What reconciles, in my mind, these two potentially conflicting ideas of a value system on which to base human decisions, is the fact that native people, when deciding what might be good for "the Seventh Generation," apparently generally took into account their interdependence with what we call "the environment." In fact, I'm suspicious that, given their apparent general feeling of being a part of Creation, they may not have even had, or often used a word for environment in many native languages.

The first ethical choice to which I refer can perhaps most easily be explained by reference to the Earth as "Spaceship," what I often call "Spaceship Gaia." In the discussions I've seen concerning environmental problems over the past 50 years, this spaceship analogy is almost universally lacking. Problems are defined, not as one would on any other spaceship, in terms of how do we live with this much water? or how do we live with this much food?, etc., but rather in terms such as how do we get MORE water? And how can we provide MORE food?, etc. Our societies tend to define many of our problems in terms of "shortages," while people on most spaceships would recognize the "longages" of excess demands on available resources, probably even before they occur.

Related to this is the fact that "Gaia has Cancer...and we are it." Continually seeking (as a group) to use ever more of the Earth's resources, and to inject increasing quantities of waste into Gaia's natural recycling systems is a form of mass suicide or, in this case, Eco- or Biosphero-cide. Malthus may have had the numbers wrong, and Ehrlich in his turn, but it's hard to imagine any scenario in which our fate is any different than any other cancer.

In fact, there are many ways in which we are destroying the Planet (probably many of which no one is even yet aware), any ONE of which might be all that is needed to eventually wipe out most or all of the Biosphere.

If you accept my premise that the survival of the Biosphere matters, and you understand that the life support system of Spaceship Gaia is just designed to support up to a certain finite amount of certain life activities, then you can probably agree with the conclusion that we should figure out just how much of our human impact can the Biosphere sustain, and then choose to see that we make plans to keep the actual amount of impact AT or BELOW that amount. (The Chinese, for example, assessed their resources some decades ago, and reached the conclusion that their available renewable fresh water supply was sufficient to sustain maybe 800 million people. They then decided to create a population plan that would attempt to reduce their population, over time, back to that sustainable figure [by definition, having a population above the sustainable number would lead to an increased death rate]).

A choice which I'm not even planning to discuss this morning is the decision to choose to have a long term human impact which is AT or BELOW that which is sustainable.

The first choice which I DO want to address is one that I've actually never even heard mentioned in any of the media (including educational institutions, books, etc.). Basically, if one decides that we ought to have a human impact which allows the Biosphere to continue indefinitely, they are then faced with a second choice as to just how close to a maximum Biospherically sustainable human impact should we operate. By this I'm not referring to the engineering question of safety margins. That is, after determining a reasonable sustainable human impact, one would most likely want to say something like "O.K., if THIS amount of human impact can be sustained in general... just HOW MUCH human impact should we plan for... taking into account the fact of bad years, etc.?" (This brings up some clear examples of how our current thinking tends to get us into various "crisis" and "natural disaster" situations, which could pretty much easily be avoided with a little broader thinking. For example, we build houses, communities, etc., in the hundred-year flood plain of river systems, and then call it a "natural disaster" when these places are destroyed on the average of every 100 years. We create a human population using 100% of the fresh water in an area in a normal year, and then call it a "water shortage" [instead of the "demand surplus" that it is] when a predictable low water year occurs.)

What I am referring to is the idea that planning for the maximum sustainable human impact of Gaia is a very anthropocentric decision. It IS, however, potentially consistent with the preservation of the Biosphere given the idea that that impact would allow the Biosphere to continue functioning indefinitely. But the next question an Ecocentrist would ask is, "Just how much of the sustainable human impact consistent with saving the Biosphere is 'Optimal'?" That is, just how much of "the Planet" should we use? This is the first question I'm putting before you today. Another way of asking it is, "How much of 'the Planet' should we leave for our fellow passengers and crew on the incredible continuing voyage of Spaceship Gaia?"

Among probably well-informed population activists, the common idea of what would constitute an anthropocentrically defined target population which might be sustained indefinitely WITH the preservation of much of the Biosphere is about one billion or two billion. This is based on answering the previous question with the assertion that humans "should" use 100% of "the Planet" (very consistent with Christian tradition and Old Testament).

Many population activists would be thrilled to see global human movement towards the acceptance of such a long-term population goal. For an Ecocentrist, the vision of a world of one billion human, using "all" of "the Planet," would simply be an alternative disaster scenario to a world in which humans choose to exceed carrying capacity, and thus create a major crash destroying most or all of the Biosphere.

The numbers given in the previous paragraph involve some assumptions about the second question I'm presenting today. Those saying that one or two billion is the maximum sustainable human population for the planet tend to be assuming a life style (consumption and waste production per capita) of a modern European. That is, with ready access to lots of goods, but with a more efficient use of resources than that which characterizes the U.S. today. If one assumes a future in which the average per capita consumption, etc. is more nearly that of a typical citizen of a "third world" country, then one could argue that we might still have a larger population (up to the current six billion?) and still "Save the Planet."

This then leads to the second question which I wish to present to you today. What I'm attempting to assert (here, in discussions on the Internet, in the Population movement, and in the world at large) is that what matters to the Biopshere (Saving the Planet), is the TOTAL HUMAN IMPACT. In order to sustain the Biosphere, we must, by definition, choose to consume resources and produce wastes at below the sustainable levels. The Biosphere doesn't care whether people have gas guzzling cars and/or 55-foot yachts. It doesn't even care if SOME people have gas guzzling cars and/or 55 foot yachts, while others live in poverty. It only cares if the total impact of all humans allows it to keep on functioning. So, once one has figured out just how much human impact the Biosphere CAN sustain indefinitely, and once one has decided just how much of that sustainable human impact we are going to allow (so as to leave some of the Planet for other creatures), the next question is about the distribution of wealth and it's about lifestyle. Though the idea of equal distribution of wealth (taking only a moment to note that human ideas of wealth pretty much routinely ignore the perspectives of other species, which are often included in the idea of wealth, and rarely considered as having any rights [like water rights for fish?]) is not necessary in discussing a scenario for "Saving the Planet," I'd also like to make that assumption for purposes of this discussion.

What it finally comes down to then is once we've decided on the total human impact which we wish to select for the indefinite future on the Planet will we choose to attempt to achieve it with small numbers of people driving gas-guzzling cars (actually not an option, since the gas will soon be gone) and having 55 foot yachts and 4,000 square foot homes? or much larger numbers of people living lives of voluntary simplicity?

My own position on this is...it doesn't matter. Saving the Biosphere matters, and it can be done under either scenario (the conspicuous consumer or voluntary simplicity). In fact, were I to find myself magically transported to a world which I shared with a stable population of ten million people living in 4000 square foot homes, I could easily imagine choosing to be the only one living in a much smaller, simpler shack, but making NO effort to convert anyone else to my lifestyle choices, since I'd be living in a world where the Biosphere was effectively protected forever. Of course, if these people were living in 4000 square foot houses, for the same reasons which motivate some people to do so today, I might wish to communicate with them out of fear for their souls, but this is an entirely separate issue from what I believe to be the prime ethical decision of our era and our species... "Saving the Planet."

I now throw the discussion open to your comments as to 1) How much of "the Planet" do you think humans "should" use? and 2) Do you think that there is an appropriate level of consumption, etc., per capita in your "ideal" world?

Want to do more to help heal God's wounded world? Here are some practical suggestions:

Howard Clinebell, Ph.D.

1. Knowing that the root causes of the ecological-justice crisis are spiritual and ethical problems, in your time of spiritual self-care, remember that today is the day for each of us to bring our lives more into harmony with the earth, to respect, protect, and love God's precious earth, our planet home. You may find it helpful to meditate on these Bible passages:

   "God saw everything that he had made and behold it was very good." (Genesis 1:31)

   "The earth is the Lord's and the fullness thereof, the world and those who dwell therein." (Psalm 24:1)

   "I brought you into a plentiful land to enjoy its fruits and its good things. But when you came in you defiled my land and made my heritage an abomination." (Jeremiah 2:7-8)

   "The land mourns and all who dwell in it languish, and also the beasts of the field, and the birds of the air, and even the fish of the sea are taken away." (Hosea 4:3)

   "Look at the birds of the air...Consider the lilies of the field, how they grow...Even Solomon in all his glory was not arrayed like one of these." (Matthew 6:26 and 29)

   "Blessed are the peacemakers, for they shall be called children of God." (Matthew 5:9)

   "Hurt not the earth, or the sea, or the trees." (Revelations 7:3)

2. Keep doing your homework by reading and studying to keep your mind and heart updated on the rapidly changing realities of health-care for yourself and your family, but also health-care for society and the earth.

3. Recognizing that your health and that of all those you love is dependent on the health of the social

and ecological environments that impact you every minute of every day, enlarge your daily self-care-for-wellness practices to make sure they include contributing to the health of the community and natural world around you!

4. Prayerfully examine your lifestyle and change those things that are not earth-friendly, including over-consumption. If you feel powerless and that one person can do little or nothing, bear this in mind—most if not all decisions we make have consequences for the precious environment—how many children we have, what we eat and drink, what and how much we drive, our purchases, our recycling, how we invest our money, our use of natural resources, our methods of waste disposal, our political decisions, etc.—they all have small but significant impacts on the health of our community's biosphere and that of the human family and God's earth.

5. Teach children, particularly your children and grandchildren, to love, respect and care for themselves by loving, respecting, and caring for the natural world upon which the well being of all living creatures (including us) ultimately depend. Remember that the health or sickness of the earth we leave for our kids and all the children of the human family as well as our future generations, is being created by the way we choose to live today. Living in earth-friendly ways is our gift to the future and to all children of all species.

6. Urge your elected officials at all levels of government to make protecting mother-father earth a top priority in all decisions. Make sure they remember all the parents of the earth, including those facing unwanted childbirth and those wanting their children to have a better life.

7. Work through your denominational, ecumenical, and interfaith programs to bring the power of religious commitment and passion to healing our planet's most profound health crisis.

8. Link hands with other earth-caring, life-loving persons in holistic wellness action by participating in and supporting financially several peacemaking, ecology, justicemaking, and voluntary family

planning groups on local, national, and international levels. Know that by supporting these groups you help protect our earth and humankind from further harm, and enhance the wellness of God's whole world!

The Place of Humanity in the Cosmos

Patricia Waak

Brian Swimme asks in the preface to his book, *The Hidden Heart of the Cosmos*, where did it all come from? My question is different. What is the meaning of human life in the midst of this awesome universe? It seems that the answers are evolving, or perhaps this is the true meaning of autopoesis, the process of self-regulating that all life goes through.

The fact that humans exist at all is a cause for celebration and part of the wonder of the story of our universe. Given the numbers and actions of people on Earth today, one must contemplate the meaning of humankind. At this point in the history of the universe, what do we contribute? It is easy to point to our destructive habits and institutions, but what joy, hope and completion do we bring?

While we physically exist on a planet in the greater universe, our minds, spirits and heart often seem to exist somewhere else. Brian Swimme asserts that humans throughout history have lost the sense of place. Or have we forgotten altogether about place, especially in the transient society we live in today?

We see ourselves as living on Earth but not as part of the Earth Community (Swimme 1996). Although our activities, and sometimes disregard, for our home planet seem to affirm this statement, there is a deeper aspect to this story. Our history points to a marked shift from a more personalized view of life to the mechanization of almost everything with the rise of the industrial revolution. Some of us even subscribe to the myth of alien seeding of Earth. That myth serves to separate humans from viewing Earth as home (Romanyshyn 1992). And if Earth is not home, why should we care for it?

The challenge of our time then is to re-examine our purpose in the universe as a species and as individuals. If one considers the barriers in our values and belief systems, the assumptions we make about who will take care of us, our relationship to nature and our responsibility to others, then the fate and perhaps the meaning of humanity offers several possibilities.

Maybe the meaning of humanity is to move through the life cycle like other species, serve a purpose in time and space, and then become extinct. Biologists see human beings as no different than a herd of deer, a flock of passenger pigeons, or a tribe of mountain gorillas. In biological terms, a population grows until it overcomes the carrying capacity of place and either it migrates or crashes. While other planets have been suggested as future homes for excess human population, the rate of migration would have to be incredible to keep pace with the current population. Some ask whether the current autoimmune disease (specifically HIV/AIDS) epidemics are not the beginning of the human species dieback. There is precedence in human history for this phenomenon, although more recent advances in technology have selectively prevented a pandemic from occurring. That is not to say as we contaminate our life support systems and develop new diseases a human dieback is impossible. What then happens to the universe's ability to reflect upon itself, an idea of the purpose of humanity posed by Catholic theologian Thomas Berry?

Scientists have discovered that the universe is expanding, an ongoing creativity. Could it be possible that we will reach a point where the universe will begin to curl back on itself? Can we assume that the expansion will move on forever? Just as humans will have to reach the limits of their capacity to sustain themselves, so there may be new limits that we have not foreseen. Perhaps the meaning of humanity is to take that reflection of the universe to its limits and then back to its beginning or somewhere in between that marks a point of sustainability. This idea does not imply stasis but rather a search in the cosmos for the space and time where all life can be sustained.

Another possibility for the meaning of humanity's expansion is to evolve our problem-solving capability. We have been prolific in finding solutions to problems and expanding our understanding of ourselves, other creatures and the universe itself. Is this a test, the completion of which will lead us to a new level of living and celebration? Part of the reason there are so many of us living today is that we have found stunning answers to diseases like smallpox. Childhood immunization alone has accounted for dramatic declines in infant mortality. While the numbers of humans may reflect our ability to harness natural resources, those same numbers challenge us to live in harmony with Earth's bounty. It becomes a physical, spiritual and psychological test. If we pass, it will be one of the greatest achievements in our history.

With this test comes an unparalleled opportunity to reflect a new story. We know that something different is emerging because all of the old systems of economics, religion and science are being challenged. Swimme states that we are all arising from the center of the cosmos. One writer says, "in the mystical vision, the universe, its center, and its origins are simultaneous, all around us, all within us, and all One" (Matthiessen 1978). The task before all of us is to tell the story of the universe, challenge the old paradigms and help the transition to the new understanding of our relationship to nature. Each of us has a piece of the answer to discover in ourselves and through each other.

What Jesus Runs Away From

From The Essential Rumi, Translated by Coleman Barks. Originally published by and used here with permission of Threshold Books.

The son of Mary, Jesus, hurries up a slope
   as though a wild animal were chasing him.
Someone following him asks, "Where are you going?
   No one is after you." Jesus keeps on,
Saying nothing, across two more fields. "Are you
   the one who says words over a dead person,
So that he wakes up?" *I am.* "Did you not make
   the clay birds fly?" *Yes.* "Who then
Could possibly cause you to run like this?
   Jesus slows his pace.

I say the Great Name over the deaf and the blind,
   they are healed. Over a stony mountainside,
and it tears its mantle down to the navel.
   Over non-existence, it comes into existence.
But when I speak lovingly for hours, for days
   with those who take human warmth
and mock it, when I say the Name to them, nothing
   happens. They remain rock, or turn to sand,
where no plants can grow. Other diseases are ways
   for mercy to enter, but this non-responding
breeds violence and coldness toward God.
   I am fleeing from that.

As little by little air steals water, so praise
   dries up and evaporates with foolish people
who refuse to change. Like cold stone you sit on
   a cynic steals body heat. He doesn't feel
the sun. Jesus wasn't running from actual people.
   He was teaching in a new way.

~

Christ is the population of the world,
and every object as well. There is no room
for hypocrisy. Why use bitter soup for healing
when sweet water is everywhere?

Meditative Commentary by Patricia Waak

Jesus is asked whether he is the one who wakes the dead. He responds, "I am." Does he make clay birds fly? He answers yes. When he is further questioned why he runs, he responds that he is running away from "foolish people who refuse to change." The poem says that Jesus was not really running but instead teaching in a different way.

Our life's work must be bound up with trying to communicate with those who do not want to hear. Waking people up to the wonder of the world they live in and their responsibility for it is what we must strive to do. When we are at our deepest despair and want to walk away, we must retreat into nature and find the resources to speak our words in a new way.

Then Rumi's words following this same passage say, "Christ is the population of the world, and every object as well." This is a profound statement to a person who works on issues of human population. The Cosmic Christ is present in each piece of creation and Rumi's words to remind us of our calling and compassion.

The mystics tell us to create the space for listening to the wisdom and vision of creation. Rumi points the way to the Cosmic Christ. A voice comes to us in the night and tells us we are alive, the Creator is here, and the emptied self will be filled.

Works Cited and Background Material

Works Cited

al-Hibri, Azizah Y. J.D., Ph.D. *Family Planning and Islamic Jurisprudence*. Address given on May 19, 1993 as part of the Panel on Religious and Ethical Perspectives on Population Issues. Prepcom II. Copyright 1993; Azizah Y. al-Hibri. www.consultation.org/consultation/azizah.htm

Armstrong, Karen. *In the Beginning*. New York: Ballantine Books, 1996.

Assante, Molefi Kete and Abu S. Abarry (eds). *African Intellectual Heritage*. Philadelphia: Temple University Press, 1996.

Associated Press Salt Lake City. (1998, December 7). "New Mormon handbook: Family size up to parents, God." *Boulder Daily Camera*. C7.

Barks, Coleman with John Moyne (translations). *The Essential Rumi*. New York: HarperCollins, 1995.

Barney, Gerald O. (Study Director). *The Global 2000 Report to the President*. Washington, DC: Council on Environmental Quality and the Department of State, 1977.

Bennett, P.M. and I.P.F. Owens. "Variation in extinction risk among birds: chance or evolutionary predisposition?" *Proceedings of the Royal Society London,* B 264:401-408, 1997.

The Book of Resolutions of the United Methodist Church. Nashville, TN: UMC, 1996.

Bratton, Susan Power. *Six Billion and More.* Louisville, Kentucky: Westminster/John Knox Press, 1992.

Breton, Mary Joy. *Women Pioneers for the Environment.* Boston: Northeastern University Press, 1998.

Brown, Noel J. and Pierre Quiblier eds. *Ethics and Agenda 21.* New York: United Nations Publications, 1994.

Campbell, Joseph. *Oriental Mythology.* New York: Penguin Book, 1976.

Campbell, Joseph with Bill Moyers. *The Power of Myth.* New York: Doubleday, 1988.

Catholics for a Free Choice. "Majority Report: Catholic Attitudes on Sex and Reproduction." *Fact Sheet No. 1.* Washington, DC: Catholics for a Free Choice, 1999.

The Centre for Development and Population Activities. *Interfaith Reflections on Women, Poverty, and Population.* Washington DC: CEDPA, 1996.

Chagnon, Napoleon A. *Yanomamo: The Last Days of Eden.* Chapter 3. New York: Harcourt Brace and Company, 1992.

Chapman, Audrey R., Rodney L. Petersen, and Barbara Smith-Moran, eds. *Consumption, Population, and Sustainability.* Washington DC: Island Press, 2000.

Chapple, Christopher Key. "Hinduism, Jainism and Ecology." *Earth Ethics*. Washington, DC: Center for Respect of Life and Environment. Vol. 10 No.1 Fall 1998.

Coward, Harold, ed. *Population, Consumption, and the Environment*. New York: State University of New York, 1995.

Coward, Harold and Daniel C. Maguire, eds. *Visions of a New Earth*. New York: State University of New York, 2000.

Denny, Frederick M. "Islam and Ecology: A Bestowed Trust Inviting Balanced Stewardship." *Earth Ethics*. Washington, DC: Center for Respect of Life and Environment. Vol. 10 No.1 Fall 1998.

Devall, Bill and Session, George. *Deep Ecology: Living As If Nature Mattered*. Layton, Utah: Gibbs M. Smith, Inc., 1985.

The Dhammapada. Translated by John Ross Carter and Mahinda Palihawadana. New York: Oxford University Press, 1987.

Durning, Alan. *How Much is Enough?* New York: W.W. Norton, 1992.

Ehrlich, Paul R. *The Population Bomb*. New York: Ballantine Books, 1968.

Eliot, Alexander. *The Universal Myths*. New York: Meridian/Penguin Books, 1976.

Engel, J. Ronald and Joan Gibb Engel. (eds). *Ethics of Environment and Development*. Tucson: University of Arizona Press, 1990.

Episcopal General Convention. *Resolutions*, 1973.

Episcopal General Convention. *Resolutions*, 1994.

Evangelical Lutheran Church in America. *A Social Statement on: Caring for Creation: Vision, Hope, and Justice*. Department for Studies of the Division for Church in Society. Evangelical Lutheran Church in America: September 1993.

Fink, Daniel B. "Judaism and Ecology: A Theology of Creation." *Earth Ethics*. Washington, DC: Center for Respect of Life and Environment. Vol. 10 No.1 Fall 1998.

Foreign Assistance Action Project. *Master the Subject*. Washington, DC: National Audubon Society, 1988.

Fox, Matthew. *A Spirituality Named Compassion*. Minneapolis: Winston Press, 1979.

Fox, Matthew. *The Reinvention of Work*. San Francisco: HarperCollins, 1994.

Gakuo, Kariuki. *Nyumba ya Mumbi*. Nairobi, Kenya: Jacaranda Designs, Ltd., 1992.

Global 2000 Study for the President.

Gore, Al. *Earth in the Balance: Ecology and the Human Spirit*. New York: Plume, 1993.

Gottlieb, Roger S. (ed.). *This Sacred Earth*. New York: Routledge, 1996.

The Green Cross Newsletter. Wynnewood, PA: Green Cross, May 1997.

Hamilton, Virginia. *In the Beginning: Creation Stories from Around the World*. New York: Harcourt Brace Jovanovich, 1988.

Harrison, Paul. *The Third Revolution: Environment, Population and a Sustainable World*. New York: St. Martin's Press, 1992.

Heschel, Susannah. "Comments from a Jewish Perspective on the United Nations Conference on Population and Development." *IN/FIRE Ethics Newsletter of the International Network of Feminists Interested in Reproductive Health*. Volume 3, Issues 3&4, 1994. www.consultation.org/consultation/hesche~1.htm

Hessel, Dieter T. "Christianity and Ecology: Wholeness, Respect, Justice, Sustainability." *Earth Ethics*. Washington, DC: Center for Respect of Life and Environment. Vol. 10 No.1 Fall 1998.

Hessel, Dieter T. and Rosemary Radford Ruether, eds. *Christianity and Ecology*. Cambridge: Harvard University Press, 2000.

Hinckley, Gordon, B. *Women of the Church*. Church of Jesus Christ of Latter Day Saints. www.mormons.org/conferences/96_oct/Hinckley_Women.htm, 1996.

Hope for a Global Future: Toward Just and Sustainable Human Development. Approved by the 208th General Assembly (1996) Presbyterian Church (USA). The Office of the General Assembly: Louisville, KY, 1996.

Hopfe, Lewis M. *Religions of the World*. 6th edition. New York: Macmillan College Publishing Company, 1994.

IECH Bureau Health Division. *Population and Birth Control; A Buddist Perspective*. Thimphu Bhutan: Ministry of Health and Education, 1994.

International Conference on Population and Development Programme of Action. New York: United Nations Population Fund, 1994.

Karenga, Maulana. *Odu Ifa: The Ethical Teachings*. Los Angeles: University of Sankore Press. 1999.

Kennedy, Paul. *Preparing for the Twenty-First Century*. New York, Random House, Inc., 1993.

King Jr., Rev. Martin Luther. "Family Planning—A Special and Urgent Concern." *Speech upon accepting the Planned Parenthood Federation of America Margaret Sanger Award May 5, 1966.* New York: Planned Parenthood Federation of America, Inc., 1991.

LeBlanc, Clark. *The Nature of Growth.* Washington, DC: National Audubon Society, 1988.

Macy, Joanna. *World as Lover, World As Self.* Berkeley: Parallax Press, 1991.

Maguire, Daniel C., S.T.D. "Poverty, Population and the Catholic Tradition." *Panel on Religious and Ethical Perspectives on Population Issues, Prepcom II.* www.consultation.org/consultation/maguire.htm. New York, May 19, 1993.

Maguire, Daniel C. and Larry L. Rasmussen. *Ethics for a Small Planet.* New York: State University of New York Press, 1998.

Martin-Schramm, Rev. James B. "Population Growth and Justice." *Panel on Religious and Ethical Perspectives on Population issues, Prepcom II.* www.consultation.org/consultation/schramm.htm New York, May 19, 1993.

Mazur, Laurie Ann (editor). *Beyond the Numbers: A Reader on the Population, Consumption and the Environment.* Washington, DC: Center for Resource Economics/Island Press, 1994.

McKibben, William. *The End of Nature.* New York: Random House, Inc., 1989.

McNeill, William H. *Plagues and Peoples.* New York: Doubleday, 1977.

Mbiti, John S. *African Religions and Philosophy.* Oxford: Heineman Educational Publishers, 1969.

Meadows, Donella H., Meadows, Dennis L., and Randers, Jorgen. *Beyond the Limits.*Post Mills, VT: Chelsea Green Publishing Company, 1992.

Merchant, Carolyn. *Earthcare*. New York: Routledge, 1995.

Miller, G. Tyler. *Living in the Environment*. Pacific Grove, CA: Brooks/Cole Publishing Company, 2000.

Myers, Norman, Russell A. Mittermeier, Cristina G. Mittermeier, Gustavo A.B. da Fonseca & Jennifer Kent. "Biodiversity hotspots for conservation priorities." *Nature* 403: 853-858, 2000.

Nash, Jim. *Manuscript and personal conversation*. Washington, DC: Churches Center for Policy and Theology, 1990.

PLANet. (http://www.familyplanet.org), 2000.

O'Connor, Archbishop John. *Earth Day News. New York Times*, 1990.

Pope John Paul II. *Crossing the Threshold of Hope*. New York: Alfred A. Knopf, 1994.

Pope Paul VI. "Humanae Vital." Encyclical Letter July 25, 1968.

Population and the American Future. Rockefeller Commission Report, 1972.

Population Reference Bureau. *2000 World Population Data Sheet*. Washington DC: Population Reference Bureau, 2000.

Population Reference Bureau. *The World of Child 6 Billion*. (http://www.prb.org/pubs/child6), 2000.

Population Reference Bureau. *Writers Forum*. (http://www.prb.org/wf/quickfacts), 2000.

Prabhupada, A.C. Bhaktivedanta Swami. *Bhagavad-Gita As It Is*. Los Angeles: The Bhaktivedanta Book Trust, 1986.

President's Council on Sustainable Development. *Population and Consumption Task Force Report*. Washington, DC: US GPO 97, 1996.

Ramphal, Shridath. *Our Country, The Planet: Forging a Partnership for Survival*. Washington, DC: Island Press, 1992.

Raven, Peter. "Why it matters." *Our Planet*. 6 (4), 1994.

Rockefeller, Steven C. and John C. Elder (editors). *Spirit and Nature*. Boston: Beacon Press, 1992.

Romanyshyn, Robert. *Techonology As Symptom and Dream*. New York: Routledge, 1992.

Rosenfeld, Bennett, Varakamin, Lauro. "Thailand's Family Planning Program: An Asian Success Story." *Family Planning Perspectives*. Vol 8, No.2, June 1982.

Ruether, Rosemary Radford. "Comments from a Christian Perspective on Religion and Population Policy." *IN/FIRE Newsletter of the International Network of Feminists Interested in Reproductive Health*. Volume 3, Issues 3 & 4, 1994. www.consultation.org/consultation/ruethe~1.htm

Schwarz, John C. *Global Population from a Catholic Perspective*. Mystic, CT: Twenty-Third Publications, 1998.

Senior, Donald (Gen. Ed). *The Catholic Study Bible*. New York: Oxford University Press, 1990.

Sjoo, Monica and Barbara Mor. *The Great Cosmic Mother*. San Francisco: Harper & Row, 1987.

Sproul, Barbara C. *Primal Myths*. New York: HarperCollins, 1991.

Stetson, Nancy and Penny Morrell. "Belonging: an interview with Thomas Berry." *Parabola*, Spring. Pp.26-31.

Strom, Kenneth. *Population and Habitat in the New Millennium*. Boulder, CO: National Audubon Society, 1998.

Swartz, Nancy Sohn. *In Our Image: God's First Creatures*. Woodstock, VT: Jewish Lights Publishing, 1998.

Swearer, Donald K. "Buddhism and Ecology: Challenge and Promise." *Earth Ethics*. Washington, DC: Center for Respect of Life and Environment. Vol. 10 No.1 Fall 1998.

Swimme, Brian and Thomas Berry. *The Universe Story*. New York: HarperCollins, 1992.

Swimme, Brian. *The Hidden Heart of the Cosmos*. Maryknoll, NY: Orbis Books, 1996.

Unitarian Universalists of America Official Website. *Population and Development 1996 General Resolution*, 10-15-99. www.uua.org/actions/population/96development.html

Unitarian Universalists of America Official Website. *Principles and Purposes*, 1997. www.uua.org/principles.html

United Methodist Church Official Website. *United Methodist Communications*. www.umc.org

United Methodist Church. *The Book of Resolutions of the UMC*. Nashville, TN: UMC, 1996.

Vitousek, Peter M., Harold A. Mooney, Jane Lubchenco, Jerry M. Melillo. "Human Domination of Earth's Ecosystems." *Science*. 277: 494-499, 1997.

Waak, Patricia and Kenneth Strom, (editors). *Sharing the Earth: Cross-Cultural Experiences in Population, Wildlife and the Environment*. Washington, DC: National Audubon Society, 1992.

Waak, Patricia. "Shaping a Sustainable Planet: The Role of Nongovernmental Organizations." *Colorado Journal of International Environmental Law and Policy*. 6.2. (1995): 342-362.

Waak, Patricia. *A Phenomenological Analysis of the Experience of Nature.* Masters thesis unpublished, 1998.

Weber, Michael, et al. *Population and Energy.* Washington, DC: National Audubon Society, 1994.

Williams, Terry Tempest, William B. Smart, and Gibbs M. Smith (editors). *New Genesis.* Salt Lake City: Gibbs Smith Publisher, 1998.

Wilson, E.O. *The Diversity of Life.* New York: W.W. Norton and Co., 1992.

Wood, Douglas. *Old Turtle.* Duluth, MN: Pfeifer-Hamilton Publishers, 1992.

World Commission on Environment and Development. *Our Common Future.* New York": Oxford University Press, 1987.

Your Church Outdoors Idea Pack. Evangelical Environmental Network. Wynnewood, PA.

Youth, H. Brown, L.R., H. Kane and D.M. Roodman. "Birds are in decline." *Vital Signs 1994.* New York: W.W. Norton and Co., 1994.

Other References

al-Hibri, Azizah, Daniel Maguire and Rev. James B. Martin-Schramm. *Religious and Ethical Perspectives on Population Issues*. Washington, DC, the Religious Consultation on Population, Reproductive Health and Ethics, May 19, 1993.

Barney, Gerald O. *Global 2000 Revisited: What Shall We Do?* Chicago, IL, Institute for 21st Century Studies, Inc., 1993.

Berry, Thomas. *The Dream of the Earth*. San Francisco, CA, Sierra Club Books, 1990.

Brown, Lester R. (editor). *State of the World* (Annual). New York, W.W. Norton & Company, 1994.

Carter, Stephen L. *The Culture of Disbelief*. New York: Basic Books, 1993.

Cleveland, Harlan. *Birth of a New World*. San Francisco, CA., Josse-Bass Publishers, 1993.

Daley, Herman E. and John B. Cobb, Jr. *For the Common Good*. Boston, MA: Beacon Press, 1994.

Diamon, Irene and Gloria Feman (editors). Reweaving the World: The Emergence of Ecofeminism. Sierra Club Books, 1990.

Dominguez, Joe and Vicki Robin. *Your Money or Your Life*. New York, Penguin Books, 1992.

Edwards, Mencer Donahue. *Population and the American Future Revisited 20 Years Later*. National Audubon Society Seminar Proceedings, 1994.

Ehrlich, Paul R. and Anne H. Ehrlich. *Healing the Planet*. Reading, MA, Addison-Wesley Publishing Co., 1991.

Ehrlich, Paul R. and Anne H. Ehrlich. *The Population Explosion*. New York, Simon & Schuster, 1990.

Eisler, Riane and David Loye. *The Partnership Way: New Tools for Living and Learning, Healing Our Families, Our Communities and Our World*. New York, HarperCollins Publishers, 1990.

Gardner, Richard N. *Negotiating Survival: Four Priorities After Rio*. New York, Council on Foreign Relations Press, 1992.

The Harwood Group. *Meaningful Chaos: How People Form Relationships with Public Concerns*. Dayton, OH, The Kettering Foundation, 1993.

Hawkin, Paul. *The Ecology of Commerce: A Declaration of Sustainability*. New York: HarperCollins Publishers, 1993.

Henderson, Hazel. *Paradigms in Progress: Life Beyond Economics*. Indianapolis, IN, Knowledge Systems, Inc., 1991.

Hynes, H. Patricia. *Taking Population Out of the Equation: Reformulating I=PAT*. North Amherst, MA, Institute on Women and Technology, 1993.

Keeping the Earth. VHS video. Narrated by James Earl Jones. Cambridge, MA: Union of Concerned Scientists, 1996.

Korten, David C. *Getting to the 21st Century: Voluntary Action and the Global Agenda*. West Hartford, CT, Kumarian Press, Inc., 1990.

Leisinger, Klaus M. and Karen Schmitt. *All Our People: Population Policy with a Human Face.* Washington, DC: Center for Resource Economics, 1994.

Long, Asphodel P. *In A Chariot Drawn By Lions: The Search for the Female in Deity.* Freedom, CA, The Crossing Press, 1993.

Meadows, Donella. *The Global Citizen.* Washington, DC, Island Press, 1991.

Montuori, Alfonson and Isabella Conti. *From Power to Partnership.* New York: Harper Collins Colleens Publishing, 1993.

"The New Face of America." *Time.* Vol. 142, No. 21, Fall 1993.

Political Environments. Vol. 1, No. 1, Spring 1994.

Population and People of Faith: It's About Time. Video and Guide, Institute for Development Training and Save the Mothers Program, Chapel Hill, NC, 1991.

Report on the Global Stewardship Survey Concerning Population, Consumption and the Environment Within the U.S. Religious Community. The North American Coalition on Religion and Ecology, Washington, D.C., Pew Global Stewardship Initiative, January 1993.

Roberts, Elizabeth and Elias Amidon (editors). *Earth Prayers.* San Francisco, CA, Harper Collins, 1991.

Sen, Gita. *Dawn: Development, Crises and Alternative Visions: Third World Women's Perspectives.* New Delhi, India: Development Alternatives with Women for a New Era, 1985.

Sen, Gita, Adrienne Germain and Lincoln C. Chen (editors). *Population Policies Reconsidered: Health, Empowerment and Rights.* Cambridge, MA, Harvard University Press, 1994.

The Social Contract. Vol. III, No. 2 Winter 1992-93.

"Special Report: Cairo Conference on Population and Development" *Audubon*. July-August 1994.

U.S. National Report on Population. Population Reference Bureau, Inc., Washington, DC, U.S. Department of State, April 1994.

USA by Numbers. Zero Population Growth, Washington, D.C., 1988.

Waak, Patricia. *Population Policy: Social Realities, Prospects and the Three Ecos*. National Audubon Society, Rosentiel Retreat, Brandeis University, May 5, 1991.

White, Robert A. *Spiritual Foundation for an Ecologically Sustainable Society*. Ottawa, Ontario, The Association of Baha'i Studies, Inc., 1993.

Winckler, Suzanne and Mary M. Rodgers. *Our Endangered Plant: Population Growth*. Minneapolis, MN, Lerner Publications Co., 1991.